PINK MOON

A Hex Support Mystery, Book 1

ANNABEL CHASE

TANA GREY

Red Palm Press LLC

CHAPTER ONE

The grandmother clock chimed twice.

"Incoming," Grace yelled. From where I had no idea. It was hard to guess when it came to my youngest sister, the whirling dervish. Spinning on a stool in the kitchen. Hanging upside down from the rafters alongside the bats in our belfry. Tormenting the ghosts at the local graveyard. All viable options for Grace Fairfield.

Elizabeth, my younger sister, emerged from the library with her nose in a grimoire so old that its pages slid to the floor as she walked. "Who's coming?"

"No clue. I'm not expecting anyone." I brushed past her to answer the door.

"Me neither." Grace's voice echoed throughout the spacious house.

I stood at the imposing wooden door and peered through the peephole that gave me a direct view of the bridge across the moat. The glass adjusted itself so that the figure was enlarged.

"It's Mrs. Diamond."

My sisters groaned in unison. Donna Diamond was our

closest neighbor, which didn't mean much when our house was located on seventy-five acres that included a lake and a forest. Still, the woman was a nuisance. Head of the Neighborhood Watch, member of the school board, and an all-around busybody, Donna Diamond disliked anything that couldn't be explained in a single sentence. It made sense that she despised us as much as she did. As witches, we defied simple explanations.

"She has Gertie," I added.

"Uh oh." Grace appeared beside me, her blond hair a disheveled mess. I didn't bother to ask what she'd been doing to acquire such a look. Grace was a Chaos Witch and, thus, always appeared to be in the middle of a science experiment gone awry.

The goat trotted beside Mrs. Diamond as calm as you please.

"Butter wouldn't melt," I mumbled.

Mrs. Diamond marched to the door and rapped with intensity, prompting me to recoil from the other side.

The door began to open.

"Not yet," I hissed.

The door stopped.

I composed myself and threw open the door with a pleasant smile. "Mrs. Diamond. How nice to see you."

She thrust the end of the leash at me. "I believe this belongs to you."

I accepted the leash with an apologetic smile. "I'm so sorry. Gertie loves to roam."

"She has plenty of space to do that here," Mrs. Diamond said in a clipped tone. "I don't see why she feels the need to pester the rest of us."

Appearing to sense she was the topic of conversation, Gertie bowed her head and dragged herself across the threshold.

"You owe me a new leash and a pair of slacks," Mrs. Diamond said. "Your animal savaged my best pair in my efforts to apprehend her."

Grace snorted. "She isn't a criminal."

Mrs. Diamond turned her attention to my youngest sister. "Assault and battery, young lady. And property damage." She dusted invisible particles from her floral top. "But I won't bother to sue. We don't all have your deep pockets." She waved a hand airily to indicate the house. "That being said, if this keeps up, I won't hesitate to object to your protected status. After all, red tape is my specialty."

"Thank you for bringing Gertie to us," I said.

"Secure your fences so it doesn't happen again. You're lucky it was only the goat this time." She pivoted on her heel and marched away, along the bridge, across the moat, and back to the Chevy Impala that she likely had parked beyond the entrance gate.

I shut the door and looked at Gertie. "What do you have to say for yourself?"

"Bleat," the goat said.

"I'll take her outside," I said. "Elizabeth, would you please call Max and ask him to check the perimeter for the broken fence?"

I guided Gertie through the house to another door that led straight into the backyard. I unhooked the leash and gave her back a playful swat.

"No more mischief, please."

The goat trotted forward and joined a few of the other animals that lingered lakeside. Mrs. Diamond wasn't kidding. It would only take one so-called vicious animal to escape and our status as a sanctuary for animals would be at risk. Little did anyone in town know that these animals were mostly former familiars—animals that had once been attached to a witch, but for a variety of reasons, were now free agents with nowhere to go. People mainly associate cats with witches, but the truth is far different. Our sanctuary included cats, of course, but also a goat, a variety of birds, a ferret, a raccoon, and even an alligator, for which the moat came in handy. Like those that boarded Noah's Ark, their goal was survival. The animals arrived through a network of people similar to the way rescue shelters operated. An underground railroad for magical creatures, if you will.

I shaded my eyes and glanced at the lake where a black swan cut across the center. Bella was a gorgeous creature and she knew it. Thanks to an identification spell, I knew that her witch had died in an unfortunate accident. After she tried to bite one too many people, she found her way to our sanctuary to live out her days gliding across the lake unless she became a lucky second familiar, but they were few and far between.

I turned back to the house and, not for the first time, was struck by its grand appearance. At nearly nineteen-thousand square feet, the gothic-meets-fairy tale structure was a sight to behold. A gated entry. Stained-glass windows. Arched doorways. Two verandas. A widow's walk. Six spires erupted from the building like rockets launching into space. The tallest tower was one hundred and twenty-six feet high. I only knew because my son decided to measure it when he was eleven. Deacon was worse than Grace when it came to raising my blood pressure.

Nobody knows exactly when the castle-like house known as Dark Hollow was originally built. Technically 'Dark Hollow' encompasses the entire estate, not simply the house. Throughout the years, however, Fairfield witches have used Dark Hollow to refer to the house itself. After all, an enchanted house requires a name as much as those who inhabit it. Some claim the house was built by a robber baron in the late nineteenth century to show off his newfound wealth, but others argue the building predates names like Rockefeller, Ford, Carnegie, and Vanderbilt. There are no public records of the structure. The truth, however, would be too difficult for most people to handle. The truth about the enchanted house, about the sanctuary animals, about my family.

All of it.

The door swung open as I approached and I re-entered the house to find Elizabeth hovering inside. She appeared to be waiting for me.

"We have a visitor," she whispered.

I frowned. "Mrs. Diamond wasn't satisfied with my response?"

My sister's face grew solemn. "Not Mrs. Diamond."

I entered the front hall to satisfy my curiosity. A recognizable figure stood beside the grandmother clock. He looked remarkably the same for a man I hadn't seen in the better part of a decade. His hair was fully silver now and his gut slightly rounded, but the eyes were the same shade of brown and his mouth still retained the shape of perpetual disappointment. In a rumpled white shirt beneath a tweed jacket, khaki trousers, and brown loafers, he wore the uniform of an absent-minded professor, although he was far from it. Disorganized, yes, but also sharp as a fang when the situation required it. In his line of work, it often did.

"Hello, Martin."

He shrugged off the tweed jacket and handed it to Grace. "I was just telling your sisters how much they've grown since I last saw them."

"Not me," Elizabeth said. "I've been this height since I was eleven."

It was true. Elizabeth was the tallest of the three of us and had begun to tower over me in adolescence.

Martin observed the grand entrance with its wood inlaid

floor and antique furnishings. "I see this place hasn't changed a bit, not that I expected anything else."

"Last time you were here, the woodwork rendered you speechless," I said.

Martin turned toward one of the false doors—windows designed to match the arched doorway. Thoughtfully he placed a hand on the trim. "Ten species of wood, wasn't it?"

"Over twenty-five," Elizabeth corrected him. "Imported from all over the world."

Martin released an impressed breath. "The beauty of this place never ceases to amaze me."

"Is that why you've come in person?" I asked.

He turned back to me. "I suppose that's one reason. Any excuse to admire it again."

"Peppermint tea?" I offered.

He smiled. He had what Grace referred to as British teeth, although I made her swear never to say it out loud again. There were plenty of British people with very fine teeth.

"You remember," he said.

"I remember a lot." I beckoned him toward me and together we walked into the formal parlor room reserved for guests of distinction. As my former boss at the Federal Bureau of Magic, Martin fit that description.

The FBM is a secret sister organization to the FBI and within the FBM is an even lesser-known division known as Hex Support. Whereas FBM agents are usually attached to a specific location, Hex Support agents go wherever they're needed. The assignments tend to be high-profile or especially delicate matters. As a Green Witch, I excelled in herbal magic, which proved a useful specialty in my line of work.

My former line of work, that is. I left Hex Support behind ten years ago and never looked back.

I sat in the stuffed armchair and left the settee for Martin.

A moment later, a tray sailed into the room and landed on the coffee table.

Martin observed the brimming teacup. "And not a drop spilled. Your house is a wonder, Kit." He lifted the cup to his lips. "Cheers. Wonderful to see you again."

I crossed my ankles. "I take it this isn't a social visit."

"No, but let's pretend for a moment that it is. How are the twins?"

"Enjoying their first year at college. Top marks for both of them."

"Same school?"

"No. Deacon is at Johns Hopkins and Imogen is at Penn."

A small smile touched his lips. "I didn't think she'd wander far from the nest, although I suppose nowhere is very far from Dark Hollow."

"It's an hour from here by car," I said. "That's far enough to develop independence, but not so far that they never visit." I felt torn between wanting them to flourish on their own and never wanting them to leave my side. A mother's conflict.

"It's good, old-fashioned cars for the twins, is it?" He seemed amused.

"I want their lives to be as normal as possible."

"They were smart kids. I'm not at all surprised where they ended up." He took another sip of tea. "I suppose you've found ways to keep busy without them."

"We have the sanctuary. That's a full-time job."

Martin grunted. "Is it? I should think between the three of you, you have it well under control."

"One would think." I uncrossed my ankles. I was anxious and trying desperately not to show it. "How's Lucy?"

"Excellent. She retired last year. Been begging me to do the same so we can take more trips together."

"Why don't you?"

"Because then we'd take more trips together." He sighed.

"I've seen enough. When I retire, I will want to switch off and become a couch vegetable."

"A couch potato? Or a vegetable?"

His brow creased. "I always thought they were the same thing."

"Close enough."

"I'll cut to the chase. We'd like you to come back to the FBM. To Hex Support. Your kids have left the nest. Your sisters are older now. You have no excuse."

I cocked an eyebrow. "Do I need an excuse?"

"It was understandable with James gone that you would feel the need to sacrifice your career..." He trailed off. Martin had never been good with expressions of emotion. I chalked it up to an adolescence spent at an English boarding school.

"I stayed home to raise my children," I said. "It wasn't a sacrifice, Martin. It was a privilege."

"Yes, of course. I didn't mean anything by it." He set the empty cup on the tray and the items were whisked away by an unseen hand.

"I find it hard to believe that the bureau is so desperate, they need to recruit women in their forties who are ten years out of the game."

"You're not simply a woman in your forties, Kit. You're a masterful witch and an excellent agent. Hex Support could use someone with your skills right now."

"Right now?" I knew my frown lines were deepening. Grace could tell me all about it later. "What's happening?"

"It isn't what's happening. It's what's happened already." He licked his lips. "Do you remember Dottie Neff?"

"The name rings a bell."

I reached into the recesses of my mind. I found it hard to remember names from my old life. I could tell you the names of my children's friends from high school—could even tell you their birthdays—but names from my professional past were largely forgotten. Intentionally.

"I'll give you a hint. Savannah."

Suddenly her file appeared fully formed in my mind.

Dottie Neff was a formidable mage with a large fortune, an even larger mouth, and a fondness for grand parties. An invitation to a party hosted by Dottie Neff was the magical equivalent of being made by the mob. It meant you were somebody in Savannah. She had a reputation for dancing too close to the legal line when it came to magic use. As a result, she'd been put on the Watch List during my tenure.

"What happened? Did she finally cross the line?"

"No, she crossed over. She's dead," Martin said.

I didn't bother to hide my shock. "What happened?"

"She threw a costume party at a place called The Mad Hatter. She was dressed as the Queen of Hearts. I'm sure you can guess the cause of death."

My fingers inadvertently reached for my neck. "Weapon?"

"To be determined."

"Witnesses."

"None. Her head was found atop a statue in the courtyard."

"A gruesome end."

He sniffed. "You're not kidding."

"Why me?"

"Aside from the fact that you're the best we ever had?"

I pulled a face at him. "No need to flatter me, Martin."

"We're in a tight spot. Our current best is on another assignment, a delicate matter involving a politician and a summoning circle gone awry. It has the potential to blow up in spectacular fashion."

"I find it hard to believe you have no one else qualified."

Martin rubbed the back of his head, a sure sign of his growing frustration and impatience. It was amazing the small details you could remember about a person you hadn't seen in years.

"They're qualified, but they're not *you*."

I knew what 'you' meant and it wasn't as straightforward as it sounded. He wanted someone the caliber of a Fairfield witch.

"I get that Dottie is a high-profile mage and that's why Hex Support is involved, but what aren't you telling me?"

Martin cleared his throat. Another detail I remembered. Whatever information he was hiding, he was determined to keep it that way.

"Nothing. We simply want this matter handled as quickly, quietly, and proficiently as possible and that means you, Kit. Dottie's murder has the potential to draw the wrong kind of attention. If we don't attend to it swiftly, before you know it there will be a supernatural swarm descending upon Savannah. It will become the Wild West."

I couldn't resist a smile. "Don't you think that might be a slight exaggeration?"

Martin slapped his hands on his thighs. He was getting desperate and ready to negotiate. "How about this? You take this one job as a favor to me. If you're interested in more work after this, we'll discuss a contract."

On the one hand, it would be nice to get out of my comfort zone. Once the twins left for college, I'd struggled to find ways to occupy my time. The kids were thriving. The plants were thriving. The animals were thriving.

But was I?

"We'll make it worth your while," he continued. "Tuition is expensive these days, or so I've heard. I know James had life insurance..."

I held up a hand. I didn't want to talk about James. "I'll do it."

Martin appeared visibly relieved. "Oh, thank the gods. I

was ready to throw in a car. This is a monumental favor, Kit. I appreciate it. I'll have my assistant send over the pertinent details. How soon can you get to Savannah?"

"I'll leave in the morning."

"Perfect. I take it you still have your usual method of travel available to you?"

"Of course."

He stood and stretched his back. "I hope this is a fruitful venture for us both. I would love to have you back on board."

"Let's not get ahead of ourselves."

"Wouldn't dream of it."

"It was good to see you again," I said, because it was true. I'd always been fond of Martin. He was the ideal mentor— patient, kind, and incredibly capable. I owed him a great deal, which was the main reason I felt compelled to agree to his request. And the extra pocket money wouldn't hurt. He was right, tuition was outrageously expensive.

Martin tipped an imaginary hat. "Good luck, Kit. I eagerly await your report."

Lights turned on automatically as I passed through each room. The house anticipated our needs and seemed to know us as well as we knew ourselves. It made life here comfortable, especially in the months following my husband's death. I'd been in my early thirties looking after Grace as well as the twins, and I had Elizabeth by my side, but it was Dark Hollow that got me through the most difficult moments. I was never frazzled or overwhelmed, at least not with tasks and chores. Emotionally was another story.

In my room, I packed an overnight bag with enough necessities to last a few days. My familiar climbed into the bag and I scooped her out.

"Sorry, Isis. Only one of us is going."

She meowed and swished her tail.

"I need you to be my eyes and ears here," I told the cat. "I haven't been away on my own in ten years. Watch Grace. Make sure she doesn't burn the house down."

Isis rubbed her black fur all over the white shirt folded on the bed.

I cemented a hand to my hip. "So it's like that, is it?"

The cat looked at me and meowed again. Plenty of witches shared a telepathic bond with their familiars, but Isis was too cool to share her thoughts with me. I chose not to take it personally.

"You'll want a cardigan," Elizabeth advised from the bedroom doorway.

I craned my neck to regard her. "It's mid-April in the deep South. I should probably pack bug spray and sunscreen."

"I checked the weather forecast. The evenings are still supposed to be chilly."

Begrudgingly I grabbed a cardigan from a hanger in the closet and tossed it on top of the pile in the bag.

Once I finished packing, I went outside to say goodbye to the animals. Amos, the pot-bellied pig, trotted toward me. He'd come to us from a wizard who suffered from pancreatic cancer and could no longer care for him. The illness had been swift and merciless. Amos had settled in nicely and was a gentle presence amidst some of the more vocal members of the sanctuary.

I caught a glimpse of Midas in the moat and waved. The alligator disappeared beneath the surface of the water. Midas came to live here before I was born, but he was as shy now as he was then. He seemed fond of Grace, though, and would sometimes swim to shore when she was outside.

Next I checked on the gardens and the potted plants on the balconies. Nothing required attention, which was no surprise given that I'd doted on them for years. They were healthy and flourishing.

Now it was my turn.

I returned to the house, looped the handle of my bag over my arm, and approached the large oil painting on the wall in the study. Not only did our house have a moat and spires, it also had a portal. Suffice it to say, these weren't features generally found in real estate listings.

"Break a leg," Grace said.

I cast a glance over my shoulder. "It isn't a performance."

"It sort of is. You'll have to pretend to be an agent."

I tensed. "I *was* an agent."

"That's the operative word right there. Was." Clasping her hands behind her back, she strolled forward. "For what it's worth, though, I think you'll be great."

"I appreciate the vote of confidence."

"It'll be good for you to get away from us. You've been in charge of Dark Hollow forever."

"It only seems like forever because you were so young when..." I stopped, unwilling to finish the sentence.

Grace threw her arms around my waist and hugged me. "Everything will be fine here. Go make the world a better place. The gods know you can't do that from Fort Fairfield." She withdrew her arms. "I'll see you soon."

I squared my shoulders and concentrated on the painting. It was a pretty depiction of the landscape surrounding Dark Hollow. A crystal blue lake and a dense green forest. A blue sky with the kind of white clouds that gave rise to the imagination.

Placing a hand on either side of the frame, I formed a connection with the portal and said, "Savannah, Georgia."

The clouds dissipated and the house folded into itself. I wasn't certain exactly where I'd end up in Georgia's fifth-largest city. The portal on our end was through the painting, but the destination would be a power point where multiple ley lines converged. Cities like Savannah that were doused in magical energy had multiple portals. When I wanted to return home, I'd have to find the nearest one. Thankfully technology had advanced since my time in the field and there was now an app called APIAS to help me identify energy pockets, including the nearest entry point. Short for Any Portal in a Storm, it was basically Google Maps for supernatural travel.

Wrought iron gates and gravestones replaced the trees and the lake of Dark Hollow. I recognized elements of Bonaventure Cemetery. The location didn't surprise me. Between the historical city and the Wilmington River, the old cemetery was teeming with magical energy.

Drawing a deep breath, I grabbed the overnight bag and walked through the gate.

CHAPTER TWO

The air in Savannah was unexpectedly chilly for mid-April. Well, unexpected except for Elizabeth's warning. Sometimes having a know-it-all for a sister wasn't such a hardship. I unzipped my overnight bag and retrieved my cardigan.

Unfortunately the cemetery was a good four miles away from downtown and public transportation wasn't an option. I pulled out my phone, intending to find an Uber, when a pickup truck pulled in front of the gate. Dirt sprayed from beneath the oversized tires as the truck slid to a halt.

The driver rolled down the window. He looked mid-thirties, with a scruffy jawline. Light brown hair poked out from beneath an Atlanta Falcons hat. "Did you know the birth flower for July is Larkspur?"

"It signifies love and joy," I replied.

The driver broke into a crooked grin. "Martin said you might end up here. Can I give you a lift?"

"That would be very helpful, thank you."

I crossed in front of the truck and opened the passenger door. Once I dropped my bag on the floor and secured my seatbelt, the driver offered his hand.

"Name's Bert."

"Katherine Fairfield," I said, shaking his hand. "I can't believe Hex Support is still using the same codes."

"Don't fix what ain't broken," Bert said. He pulled the truck onto Bonaventure Road and headed toward the heart of the city.

"You know the drop-off location?" I asked.

"'Course. Wouldn't be very good at my job if I didn't." He gave me a cursory glance. "If you don't mind me asking, why'd you introduce yourself as Katherine Fairfield?"

"Because that's my name."

"Aren't you an agent?"

Laughter caught in my throat. He was right. "I'm a little out of practice."

"Seems to me you earned that title whether you've been on hiatus or not. You ought to use it."

Hiatus. That was one word for it. "Thank you for the reminder. I'll keep it in mind."

Bert turned onto a side street and parked. "This is where you get off." He pointed. "Number 42 is where you're headed."

I glanced across the street at the three-story building. Dense ivy managed to camouflage six sets of tall, green shutters. It didn't seem like the kind of place the bureau would use for a safe house. Then again, I'd been out of work for ten years so what did I know?

"Know anything about it?" I asked.

"Well-run. The owner understands the assignment."

I turned to look at him. "And you?"

"Oh, I understand the assignment, too. You won't be seeing me again unless you need me."

"Like Nanny McPhee."

He frowned. "Who's that?"

"Never mind." Too many years at home had reduced me

to pop culture references for kids' movies. At least it wasn't Barney.

"I mean if you're in dire straits," Bert continued. "You don't plan on being in dire straits, do you? Because I've got a flag football game this weekend and it's practice, practice until then."

"I have no intention of being in dire straits."

He nodded. "Glad to hear it. Good luck, Agent Fairfield."

I exited the truck with my bag and crossed the quiet road. A rickety wooden sign on the partial brick wall identified the building as The Springhouse.

A wrought-iron knocker in the shape of a horned skull greeted me. I knocked on the door and waited. The door was answered by a short, sturdy woman swathed in a green and pink floral maxi-dress. She had the kind of unlined face paired with soulful brown eyes that made it impossible to guess her age.

"Good morning. I'm Agent Katherine Fairfield. Martin sent me."

She regarded me coolly. "I don't know anyone called Martin." She started to close the door.

I quickly wedged my foot between the door and the jamb. "The ants go marching two-by-two," I blurted.

Her expression gave nothing away. "The little one stops to tie his shoe."

Relief washed over me. It was obvious to me now that I hadn't prepared for this assignment as much as I should have. Thankfully the memories were coming back to me, albeit in fragments.

"Miss Lemonte?"

She opened the door and ushered me inside. "You may call me Madam."

"Madam?" My gaze swept the homey interior of the

house. A fully stocked china cabinet. Overstuffed chairs. Newspapers.

The woman's laughter tinkled like a bell. "Not to worry, mon cher. The Springhouse isn't a brothel."

"Sorry, in my line of work those were the only madams I ever encountered."

"Understood." She clapped her hands together. "Oh, I'll be telling this story at mahjong tonight. A brothel." She chuckled to herself. "Would you like a cup of tea before I show you to your room?"

"Why not?"

I followed her to the parlor room where a teapot and two teacups were already waiting for us.

"I took the liberty of brewing it ahead of time. English breakfast, yes?"

"Yes." I set my bag on the floor and perched on the edge of a wingback chair.

"This is more than a safe house for you, Agent Fairfield. If you need anything at all during your stay, you need only ask."

I blew the steam off the surface of the tea before taking a sip. One sugar. A tablespoon of milk. It was perfect.

"Are there any other guests?"

"Not at the moment, no."

Good. I didn't need any other witnesses as I fumbled my way through my first assignment in a decade.

"I have an appointment today with a lawyer named George Mahon? Do you know him?" Martin had texted me the information before I left. He thought the lawyer seemed like a good starting point.

"Everybody in town knows George. He handles all the high-net worth estates in the area."

"I assume you know the reason I'm here."

Her expression turned grim. "A dreadful affair."

"Did you know the victim?"

"No, but I knew of her. Dottie Neff was a fixture in Savannah. Big money and big mouths generally garner attention."

I drained my teacup and set it on the saucer. "Thank you. That hit the spot."

"It's unseasonably chilly today. It's a good thing you wore an extra layer."

I glanced at my cardigan. "Yes. It is."

She placed her cup on the table and rose to her feet. "Why don't I show you to your room?"

I trailed behind her as we made our way through the maze-like layout of the house.

"I'm guessing the interior has been modified over the years," I remarked as I climbed a narrow staircase to the third floor.

"Here and there."

She stopped in front of a wooden door painted off-white. "The Executive Suite."

"Thank you." I maneuvered past her and entered the room. A four-poster, canopied bed made the room appear smaller than it actually was. The oversized dresser didn't help.

"Please let me know if you require anything else. Breakfast is promptly at eight and the keys to your room and the front door are on the nightstand." She closed the door and left me alone.

I unpacked the few items I'd brought and put them in the dresser drawers. The only thing I transferred to my handbag was my notebook. I didn't care how far technology had advanced or how much my sisters would mock me if they knew, I wasn't taking notes on a phone. Pen and paper only.

I glanced at the clock on the nightstand. It was almost time for my meeting with the victim's lawyer. I was hopeful he could offer an overview of Dottie's friends and enemies, as well as any possible motives for her murder.

I grabbed the keys and walked the three flights to ground level. Too bad I hadn't brought my Fitbit. I'd get my ten thousand steps in here without a problem, not that I had trouble at home. One circuit visiting all the animals in the sanctuary and I'd logged more than I needed. Over the years we'd discussed hiring someone to look after the animals full-time, but we never pulled the trigger. We knew that as much work as the sanctuary was, we got more out of it than we put in and we were loath to give it up. That included my daily steps.

I left the safe house and strolled along the picturesque streets toward the lawyer's address on East Bryan Street. Between the cobblestone streets, manicured gardens, and Spanish Moss glinting from the thick branches of live oaks, Savannah was one of the prettiest American cities I'd had the pleasure of visiting. Too bad the reason for this visit was so ugly.

I found the lawyer's office and headed inside. The receptionist didn't even offer me a seat. She simply waved me right in. I had to imagine the lawyer was anxious. It wasn't every day one of your best clients loses her head, not literally anyway.

George Mahon was a burly man, built like a retired football player. His bald head was so smooth that it caught the artificial light from above. He wore a light grey suit with a pink bowtie.

He shot to his feet when I entered the office. "You must be Ms. Fairfield. I'm George Mahon, Ms. Neff's attorney."

I shook his hand. It was cool, firm and dry, like a stone in the evening desert. "Agent Fairfield," I corrected him, remembering Bert's comment. I had to admit, it felt odd to refer to myself as an agent again when I'd been mostly 'Mom' or 'Kit' for a decade, but he was right. I'd earned the title. "I'm sorry for your loss."

"Thank you. Please have a seat. Can I get you anything? My secretary brought macarons today and they're out of this world."

"No, thank you." I sat in the burgundy leather chair across from the desk. The surface was covered in paperwork and I couldn't decide whether George Mahon was overworked or disorganized—maybe both.

"I imagine you're here to ask me about who might've killed Dottie."

"That's one of my questions, yes."

Nodding, he pursed his lips. "The whole thing was quite unexpected. You think a woman like Dottie will live forever."

"Death is one thing we all have in common, Mr. Mahon." I withdrew my notebook from the handbag and rooted around for a ballpoint pen. Blue ink. I was very particular when it came to writing implements. "I understand Dottie had a certain reputation in town."

"You mean because she was loud and boisterous? Depends on who you ask. She was always good as gold in this office, although I know she was banned from a couple local restaurants for dressing down the chefs after a substandard meal. She wasn't afraid to speak her mind, that Dottie." He heaved a sigh. "They broke the mold when they made her, bless them."

"Tell me about the event where the incident took place. I'm told it was a party?"

"Not just a party. A Mad Hatter's tea party," he clarified. "Very exclusive."

"A tea party? I'd expect more from a woman with a larger-than-life personality."

"Oh, this was no ordinary tea party, my dear." He leaned forward with sparkling green eyes and whispered, "It's one of the few events of the year where magic is permissible."

"I see."

He suddenly seemed to remember he was speaking to a federal agent. "She received a provisional license from the local council, of course. Everything was above board. I saw to it myself."

"Did you attend the party?"

His head bobbed. "Yes, naturally. Dottie...Ms. Neff treated her staff like family. She included everyone from her PR rep to her personal assistant."

"You can call her Dottie if you like. I won't think of you as less professional if you do." In fact, I'd like him that little bit more. He reminded me of the Fairfield family lawyer. Nobody knew exactly how long Gus Abernathy had been practicing law, but I'd seen his signature on paperwork dating back to my grandmother's marriage certificate.

"I appreciate that," George said.

"I'd like a list of names. Guest list as well as staff."

"The guest list is confidential, I'm afraid, but I can give you the list of staff members."

I offered a pleasant smile. "The guest list isn't confidential to me, Mr. Mahon."

He eyed me for a moment. "No, I suppose it isn't. Even so, I don't have access to it. You'll have to ask Mandy, that's her assistant."

I wrote 'Mandy' on the list. "Last name?"

"Hubert."

"Any idea where I might find her?"

"Easy. She lives in the guest cottage on my client's estate."

Another note. "What can you tell me about the will?"

"Nothing until it's been read to the relevant parties. The envelope has a magic seal. I can't open it until the relevant people are in the room."

"And when do you expect that to happen?"

He consulted his phone. "The twenty-first at five o'clock. It'll last about two hours max."

"Then I guess I'll see you Thursday at seven. Don't make plans for an after-party." I added the date and time to my planner.

"You might want to try adapting to technology," George said. "I find it incredibly helpful in my line of work."

"I'm old school." I pictured my kids mocking my use of pen and paper for reminders and the school's paper calendar attached to the side of the refrigerator. I wasn't an early adopter by any stretch of the imagination. I wasn't even a late adopter. I mainly ignored technological leaps and bounds, except apps that identified portals. Those were indispensable unless you had a fondness for public transportation, which I did not.

I decided to placate him. "I'm sure you're right. I just can't seem to bring myself to learn new tricks. This old dog is content with things as they are."

"I suppose you rely on magic anyway, as witches are wont to do."

I looked at him askance. "What makes you think I'm a witch?"

"I may be a boring, old human, but I've had enough magical clients to develop a good idea of who's who and what's what."

"Like Dottie?"

George made an effort to tidy the loose papers on his desk. "Oh, yes. She loved to use magic at every permissible opportunity. She comes from a long line of mages, you see, and she was the most powerful of the current crop. There always seems to be one superstar in each generation of Mulgrews—that's her mother's side of the family. It's the reason her events were so important to her. They gave her a chance to show off. I remember one year she turned all of the catering staff into rabbits." He slapped his leg. "It was delightful."

I doubted it was delightful for the catering staff.

"Did your client do that a lot? Use magic on others without their consent?" Could be a motive for murder. Humiliate the wrong person and you end up with your head on a statue.

George frowned. "It was all in good fun, I assure you."

"I don't doubt that was her point of view. Maybe someone at the receiving end of it had a different opinion." I glanced at my notes. "Did she use a spell on party guests or staff at the tea party?"

George's expression went blank. "Not that I recall."

I'd pushed him too far. He wasn't about to rat out his client, no matter how incapable she was of getting angry with him. He was loyal, I'd give him that.

"Any signs that she's clinging to this earthly plane?" I asked. Not all magical beings were like Fairfield witches, but it seemed important to ask.

He shook his head. "If Dottie were haunting Savannah, I'd know about it."

I smiled. "She wasn't a shrinking violet, was she?"

"Not in the least. She'd have played multiple pranks by now." George gazed wistfully over my shoulder. "I can imagine her gliding around Magnolia Hall scaring the pants off prospective buyers." He chuckled. "It's a shame, really. She would've made a splendid ghost."

"Magnolia Hall is for sale?"

"Not yet. I suppose that depends on the outcome of the will."

"Didn't you draft the will?"

"Yes, but I can't possibly recall the details. She had a tendency to make changes, and with seven cousins, as well as a coterie of friends and employees..."

"It's a lot to remember."

"Indeed."

"Any recent changes?"

"No. I had my secretary check and last year was the most recent. I don't recall the reason. It varied with Dottie. Sometimes it was because the head of the museum looked at her the wrong way at the charity ball. That sort of thing."

"You mean spite." I wrote down 'no recent changes to will.' "I'd like to look around the house, if you wouldn't mind."

"Mandy can help you with that. She has access to the entirety of the estate, not simply the guest cottage."

"Nice work if you can get it."

"Dottie was generous with those who were loyal to her."

"Mandy was paid to be loyal, no? In my experience, there's a difference."

George rubbed his chin. "I can see your point. I would consider myself quite loyal to her, though I'm not certain if I'd feel that way had she fired me." He paused, appearing to consider the possibility. Then he looked at me with a sad smile. "Guess I'll never know."

CHAPTER THREE

Magnolia Hall was every bit as glitzy and glamorous as I expected. The floor was glossy black marble with flecks of gold. The dramatic decor looked straight out of a catalogue for wealthy Eighties divas. If there was a Joan Collins Collection, Dottie Neff undoubtedly owned the whole shebang.

Mandy Hubert, on the other hand, looked like an adult Girl Scout. With her high ponytail, collared shirt, khaki shorts, and sandals, she stood out like a brown paper bag on the floor of Versailles.

"Miss Hubert, thank you for meeting with me. I'm Agent Fairfield." I shook her hand. "I'm sorry for your loss."

"Thank you for saying that. Do you know you're the only one?" She squeezed my hand before releasing it. "People seem to think that just because I worked for Dottie that I've got no right to care she died, but her death has me as shook as if she were my own kin."

"I'm sure. You were her personal assistant and you live in her backyard. You'd have to be a robot not to be impacted by her death."

She wiped a stray tear from her cheek. "I keep expecting

her to waltz through the door and yell 'surprise.' She liked to play practical jokes."

"That's what George Mahon said as well." I surveyed the grand foyer. "Is there somewhere more comfortable we can talk? This will take a few minutes."

Mandy snapped to attention. "Oh, yes. Of course. Right this way."

She guided me to an office. At least I assumed it was an office. Between the marble bust, the black and white geometric wallpaper, and the silky mauve upholstery, the only item that suggested 'office' was the lacquer desk.

"You're with the Federal Bureau of..." She left the last word dangling.

"Magic," I finished for her.

She sank against the mauve chair. "I was hoping you'd say that. I've never met anybody from the FBM before. My father has a friend from college who works for the FBI, though. I always thought it sounded so cool. I guess it's dangerous."

"It can be, depending on the division."

Her gaze turned to rest on the marble bust and I started to suspect it was Dottie. "I've never known anybody who died before. It's been real hard."

"Death is inevitable, Ms. Hubert, and yet we still struggle to make peace with the fact that it happens. It's the human condition." I used the term 'human' loosely, of course.

Mandy fixed her innocent eyes on me. "I guess you have experience with that."

"More than I care to." An image of James flashed in my mind and I quickly squelched it. When Martin first offered me the job, I worried my past would come back to haunt me. Then again, I'd have to be a robot not to be impacted by his death—even now. I decided to cut myself some slack.

"My parents think I should move back home, that

Savannah is too dangerous." Her lips formed a pout. "My momma thinks it's because Dottie used too much magic. She has a blame-the-victim mentality."

"Your mother doesn't approve of magic?"

"Momma's a fairy, but my daddy's human so she don't use magic. Thinks it makes their marriage stronger to be on equal footing." She shrugged. "I didn't inherit any magic, so I don't need to worry about any of that."

"Sounds like your mother didn't hide her true nature though."

"Not from us. I mean, she don't announce it to the neighbors, of course, because they're all humans. Anyway, it's one of the reasons Dottie hired me. She needed someone familiar with the supernatural world but who also had the necessary discretion when dealing with the human population."

"It seems that Dottie didn't exercise much discretion herself. She was a fan of showing off her magic."

The hint of a smile graced Mandy's lips. "Showing off is putting it mildly. She loved everything about being a mage. She would've used magic all over Savannah in broad daylight if she could've gotten away with it."

I steered the conversation where it needed to go. "Which is why she liked to throw magical parties."

"For sure. She'd get itchy between events, too. Always wanted to get another party on the calendar so she had something to look forward to. Another excuse to use magic in front of others. My momma says it isn't polite to flaunt your magic. She thinks Dottie..." She trailed off.

"She thinks Dottie deserved what happened to her?"

"She said that if Dottie had been content to use magic in the privacy of her own home and not be such a big shot that she'd still be alive today."

"We don't know that, not without knowing who killed her

and why. On that note, I assume you have a copy of the guest list for the tea party."

Mandy blinked back tears. "I do, but I can't give you that. It's confidential. Dottie said to treat it like a secret treasure."

"Under the circumstances, I think Dottie would want you to hand it over." I shifted forward on the chair. "I could get a warrant, Mandy, but between you and me it's a real headache. I'm pretty unpleasant when I have a headache. Ask my kids. They'll tell you."

Mandy plucked an invisible thread on her shorts. "I don't know."

"You want to find out who killed Dottie, right?"

She nodded vigorously.

"And the killer is very likely someone on that list."

"I guess so." Mandy's cheeks became tinged with pink. "It's just that I'll feel so guilty. Dottie made me swear to never, ever reveal the guest list to anyone. I even had to swear an oath."

"Why the need for secrecy? Once everyone is at the party, isn't it easy to figure it out?"

"Everyone's in costume," she explained. "That's half the fun. There's a sense of anonymity. You can be as hidden as you want."

"But not Dottie."

Mandy blew a raspberry. "Definitely not. Dottie wanted everyone to know who she was. She dressed as the Queen of Hearts, but no mask. She left her face visible."

"What did you dress as?"

Mandy seemed taken aback by the question. "Me?"

"You were there, weren't you? George said Dottie issued invitations to all her staff."

"Yes, she did. It's just that I..." She lowered her gaze. "I dress to fade into the background, I guess. I'm not accustomed to being noticed. The only time people are interested in me is when they want something from Dottie."

"I suppose that makes you the Cheshire Cat."

Her eyes widened. "That's right. I *was* the cat. Dottie conjured a spell to make my body invisible. I was basically a floating head." She grimaced. "Oh, gods. The irony."

I had the same thought. "Did anyone recognize you?"

"No, my head was designed to resemble the cat's. I even had that huge grin." A soft sigh escaped her. "We had such fun creating the costume. When Dottie was in a good mood, the energy in the whole house changed."

"Was it the same when she was in a bad mood?"

Mandy glanced away. "I guess you could say that."

"Would you say she had a temper?"

"Everybody has a temper," she said defensively.

"I'm not asking you to gossip about her, Miss Hubert. I'm trying to gather information to understand Dottie better. The more I understand the victim, the better chance I have of identifying her killer. If she blew off steam at the wrong individual..."

Nodding, Mandy chewed her lip. "That makes sense." She hesitated. "I'm the one who found her, you know. Well, I found her body first. It's one thing to murder her in cold blood, but whoever did it must've really hated her to put her head on a statue like that. It was extra spiteful."

My chest constricted at the thought of Imogen or Deacon finding a headless corpse. I felt a pang of sympathy for Mandy. "I'm sorry. That must've been very difficult for you."

"It was." Her head dipped forward, causing strands of caramel-colored hair to fall in her face. It was easy to see how she blended into the background. "I have nightmares about it."

"I can imagine. I'm sorry."

She peeked at me through the loose strands of hair. "How many dead bodies have you seen in your career?"

"Not too many. I usually get brought in after-the-fact. Like now."

Mandy opened the bottom drawer of the desk. "Let me get you that guest list."

I exhaled gently. The list would be a big help in identifying suspects.

"You knew Dottie well. Do you have any thoughts about who might've killed her?"

Mandy handed me a manila envelope. "I can think of plenty of people who might've been happy she was dead, but no one who would..." She swallowed hard. "No one who would be that cruel and vicious."

"Thank you for this." I tucked the envelope into my bag. "Would you mind showing me around? It might help me get a better picture of Dottie if I can see how she lived."

She blew her nose. "Of course. Right this way."

We left the office and meandered through the cavernous rooms. Dottie appeared to have a fondness for mirrors. I counted ten of them downstairs.

"I don't suppose you know what will happen to all of Dottie's belongings." It was going to be quite a job to pack up a house with so much *stuff*.

"I think most of it will be lumped in with the estate, but there are a few items she had earmarked for her cousins."

"Anything of substantial value?" Maybe one of the relatives wanted to get their hands on money sooner rather than later.

"I honestly don't know."

Mandy continued walking as I paused to admire an enormous gilded mirror on the wall in the entrance hall. I pictured Dottie standing here admiring her reflection on her way to the tea party. If she'd known it would be her last day on earth, would she have done anything differently? These were the kinds of questions that started to nag at me after James died. No wonder I'd opted for early retirement. Unanswered questions like that could drive you crazy if you let them.

Mandy seemed to realize I'd stopped and turned to face me. "Have you already been to the scene of the crime?"

"Not yet. It's next on my list. Were you alone when you found her?"

"I was. I went to check the courtyard to make sure the outdoor area was clear of magical residue. The Mad Hatter charges extra if you leave evidence of magic behind at your event."

"The local council seems to do a good job of keeping magic in check."

"They sure do," Mandy said. "Dottie complained about all the red tape, but she told me that if it weren't for the restrictions, it would be like every day was your birthday and that was no fun at all." Heaving a sigh, she clasped her hands in front of her. "I'd like to get the reading of the will out of the way. I need to know if I'm going to be homeless."

"Dottie didn't tell you her intentions for the guest cottage?"

"Not the guest cottage, not the house, nothing." Mandy shrugged. "She only trusted George with information like that. All I did was keep an inventory list."

"Any idea where you'll go if you can't stay here? Back to live with your parents?"

Mandy shook her head. "My sister lives in Hilton Head. I have a room there if I want it, although I'd hate to leave Savannah. I consider this my home now."

I found it hard to believe she didn't have enough money saved for a security deposit and first month's rent on an apartment. It sounded like she'd been living rent-free and was paid well by Dottie.

"I could find another job, I guess. If I find one fast enough, I'd be able to rent an apartment, but nobody will rent to me if I'm unemployed."

A valid point.

She gazed at the floor. "Dottie would've written me the most glowing reference, too. Now I'll have nothing to show for my time here."

Between the rent-free cottage and the coveted job, it seemed Mandy had every reason to want her employer alive and well. Even with a motive, I couldn't see the sweet assistant wielding the weapon that killed Dottie.

"I'm sorry, Mandy. I hope things turn around for you soon."

Her smile seemed forced. "I'm young. I'll bounce back. Dottie always said it was one of the perks of youth, having the time to course-correct."

"I know what she means." I always made a point of telling the twins that most decisions could be undone. I didn't want them to stick with a path that no longer served them simply because they'd started on it.

Closing my notebook, I was beginning to wonder if it was time to take my own advice.

CHAPTER FOUR

The Mad Hatter was within walking distance of Magnolia Hall, so I took advantage of the beautiful spring day. As I turned the corner, I realized a man had fallen in step beside me. A cursory glance told me he was tall with broad shoulders and dark blond hair. Even from this vantage point, I could tell his suit was expensive. The Gucci loafers supported my supposition. He continued to walk beside me as though we were on our way somewhere together.

"What do you think you're doing?" I asked, continuing to walk at the same pace.

The stranger acted as though he hadn't heard me.

I adopted a parental tone. "Excuse me. I am speaking to you."

That got his attention. "I thought we were headed to The Mad Hatter. Did I get that wrong?"

I ground to a halt. "We? I don't even know who you are."

He sauntered forward without answering my question. Unbelievable.

I hastened my steps to catch up to him. "*I* am going to

The Mad Hatter, but I have no idea why you think we'd be going there together."

"And here I thought you were the best of the best." He clucked his tongue. "I should've known it was an exaggeration."

I gaped at him. "Whatever happened to catching more flies with honey?"

He adjusted his cufflinks as he walked. "Is that how you plan to catch the murderer? Because I'm not sure that's a viable strategy."

My reaction was both ingenious and immature. I focused on a plant that had broken through the cracks of the pavement. There was just enough there to do the trick. I formed a connection with the plant and tugged. The long, thin roots slithered from the ground and wrapped around the man's loafer. It was the Green Witch equivalent of tying someone's shoelaces together. The man tripped and I seized the opportunity to surge ahead. I hurried through the open gates and along the pathway that led to The Mad Hatter.

As I opened the front door, I spared a glance over my shoulder. There was no sign of the mysterious stalker. I closed the door behind me and locked it for good measure. If he intended to join me, he might not make it until the interview was over. I'd have to ask Martin about him later, although I couldn't imagine why the bureau would send a second agent. The whole point of begging for my involvement was because they were short-staffed.

I took a moment to catch my breath and scan the entrance hall. If Dottie's house reflected Eighties drama, this place was Wonderland. Glowworms hung from the ceiling. A giant red and brown mushroom stood to my left. A statue of a white rabbit napped in an enormous teacup. The floor was a black and white checkerboard pattern reminiscent of Dottie's office. Frenetic music played in the background. I felt dizzy just standing here.

A figure emerged from a corridor on the right and I squinted at him to regain my focus. Admittedly I wasn't expecting an actual Mad Hatter, at least during non-tea party hours. He wasn't a hair over five-three, although his sparkly purple hat put him closer to five-eight.

"Mr..." I cleared my throat, uncertain how to address him.

"Hatter." He flicked the brim of his hat. "You may call me Mad."

I took in his ruffled shirt and brightly colored plaid trousers. His shoes were the most interesting part of the ensemble. Bulbous and red like clown shoes, they lit up with each tap of his foot.

Mad was one word for him.

"I'm Agent Fairfield from the Federal Bureau of Magic."

His eyes brightened. "The most magical of bureaus. Delightful. I have an old friend who'll work there until the bitter end. Do you know Quinn Redmond?"

I ignored the rhyme. "I'm afraid not. I work in a special division and we don't tend to mix with other agents." And I wasn't about to mention my decade-long hiatus from the bureau.

"Too bad. So sad. He's a wonderland fella." He laughed. "I mean wonderful. Why don't we retreat to my office and have a seat?" He turned to the corridor on the right and motioned for me to follow.

The office was every bit as psychedelic as the entrance. There was a tree in each corner of the room with branches that twisted across the ceiling. Colorful teacups dangled from the branches.

He patted the top of a chair upholstered in a deep shade of purple velvet. "Have a seat, Agent. I assume you're here to discuss recent events." He paused thoughtfully. "Agent and event sort of rhyme."

"We can dispense with the rhymes for the purposes of the investigation, Mr. Hatter." And for the purposes of my sanity.

As I sat, a large red and green bird squawked at me from a gilded cage in the corner of the room. "What kind of bird is that?"

"That's Icarus. He's a macaw."

"He's big."

"One of the largest pet bird species with a powerful beak. Sometimes he likes to use it to escape from his cage." He wagged a finger at the bird. "Naughty boy, Icarus."

The macaw squawked.

"Tell me about the party. I understand this was a selective event."

"Oh, indeed. I should've known better than to host during a Pink Moon, but Dottie insisted. She wanted her magic to be at its zenith during the month. She was all about maximizing her abilities."

"Yes, she was a bit of a showoff."

"I'm not one to talk." He waved a hand airily around the room. "Clearly I'm fond of maximizing as well."

"We tend to only get called in after a full moon," I said. I used to mark them on the calendar, along with doctor's appointments and the children's schedules. Everybody in the family knew not to schedule anything of importance in the few days following a full moon. After James died, of course, the full moon ceased to be a priority. I gave up my job to focus on the twins and not much else. Although I couldn't bring back their father, I could be the best mother I could possibly be. I owed them at least that much.

"Where exactly did the party take place? Was the entire building accessible to the guests?" The interior was two stories and five thousand square feet according to public records.

"The guests were mostly confined to the Alice Room, although they were free to roam the foyer and the courtyard."

"Would it be possible to see them?" I held up my notebook. "I'd like to jot down some notes as we go."

The Mad Hatter was happy to oblige.

The walls of the Alice Room were painted the shade of pale blue that the twins actually called 'Alice blue' in honor of the main character's dress. A single long table took pride of place in the cavernous room. More tea pots and cups dangled above our heads.

Mad spread his arms wide. "This is where the magic happens—or happened, in the case of Dottie Neff."

I surveyed the room. "How many guests were in attendance?"

"Thirty-three if you include the hostess. This was one of Dottie's smaller affairs. They were always exclusive, but some were more so than others. Someone like Marion Butterfield, on the other hand, fills this room to capacity because she can't bring herself to exclude anyone. Last time I was forced to remind her of the fire safety code and the hefty fine that comes with ignoring it."

"Did Dottie always pay her bills on time?"

"Oh, indeed. She paid upfront every time. Payment was never a concern."

"Who was your primary contact for Dottie's event?"

"Dottie herself, of course. And her assistant. Sandy."

"Mandy."

He snapped his fingers. "Yes, of course. Mandy. Would you like to see a menu from the party? I save a menu from every event here."

"I'll take any information you can provide."

"Wonderful. I'll be right back." He darted from the room,

which gave me an opportunity to look around without interruption.

I walked along the perimeter of the room, making notes of whatever I saw. I'd learned that sometimes seemingly unimportant objects could become important later on. The murder weapon still hadn't been found. Maybe it was right here in this very room, hidden in plain sight.

Upon further inspection, I didn't see anything here sharp enough to separate Dottie's head from the rest of her. The most dangerous item in view was the heavy furniture, which would've resulted in blunt force trauma rather than a severed head.

"Here it is." Mad returned to the room and handed me the placard. In the background was a watermark of a sword slicing through the horns of a stag.

"What's this?" I asked, tapping the symbol.

"Her family insignia, of course. All the best magical families have one."

He was right, of course. The Fairfields had a crescent moon and star as theirs. Their image was sewn and drawn on countless objects in Dark Hollow, including bedsheets and kitchen linens. When the twins were born, a distant cousin delivered matching onesies with the signifier embroidered on the backsides. When I'd remarked it was over the top, James had laughed and told me not to be such a curmudgeon. He'd always been more comfortable with the whole Fairfield legacy. He'd been the first man I met who wasn't intimidated, which was probably the reason I'd agreed to a first date with him— quickly followed by a second. Our wedding took place on the first anniversary of that first date. James was surprisingly sentimental, a quality I hadn't expected from a fellow agent.

"Were many family members at the party?"

"I couldn't say exactly. I only know the number of guests rather than their identities."

I consulted the list Mandy had given me, searching for matching surnames. I didn't see any other Neffs.

"Was it Dottie's idea to have a costumed tea party or is that typical of your events?"

"No, the costumes are...were all Dottie. She thought costumes added a touch of mystique to the ambience."

The wild decor seemed like quite enough ambience to me, but what did I know? The last party I hosted involved paper plates with images of soccer balls. The twins both loved soccer, one of the few things they agreed on.

"I'd like a list of the employees that worked the event."

"That's simple enough. The only one that wasn't on my payroll was the bartender, Jack."

"Bartender? I thought it was a tea party."

The Mad Hatter's lips parted. "All good tea parties require a mimosa or two, wouldn't you agree?"

"Why wasn't Jack on your payroll?"

"Because he was one of Dottie's regulars. She insisted on Jack for any event she hosted, whether at her residence or elsewhere."

Interesting. "Is he one of the cousins?"

The Mad Hatter grunted. "Heavens to Betsy, no. Jack is just very good at what he does. His services are in high demand, so if you're at a soiree where Jack Barnes is tending bar, you know it's the party of the season."

I wrote 'Jack Barnes' in my notebook. "Any idea where I can find Mr. Barnes when he isn't stirring and shaking?"

"There's a speakeasy called Revolution. You can usually find him there."

"Thanks."

"Anything else, Agent Fairfield?"

"Yes, one more thing. I'd like to see the courtyard where she was found."

His jaw set. "Property damage was an unfortunate consequence of the hideous act. I'll never be able to repair the statue to its former glory. I'll have to order a new one at great expense."

He exited the Alice Room and I followed behind him, trying to ignore the flashing lights of his red shoes as he walked.

The courtyard was compact and beautifully manicured. There was a statue in each corner of the square and each side was lined with shrubbery.

"This is the Four Seasons courtyard," Mad said. "Autumn, Spring, and Summer survived. As you can see, Winter was our sole victim. The killer chopped off her head in order to replace it with Dottie's." He shook his head. "Terribly sadistic. I'd like to know who the killer is if only so I can request compensation. I'd hate to take it from the estate, but it might be my only recourse."

I moved to stand in front of the headless statue. The stone figure wore an ankle-length dress, boots, and a fur collared coat over top. The neckline was surprisingly jagged, not at all the clean break I expected. I felt mildly ill thinking about Dottie.

"Where's the head of the statue now?"

"The police took it as evidence. I'd like it back when the case is solved. Even if I can't restore her, I'd like to keep it as a bust in my office." He removed his hat to wipe his sweaty brow. "Her sisters will have to do until I can find a suitable replacement."

I glanced at the trio of statues across the courtyard. Too bad they were made of stone. If her sisters could talk, they'd be able to tell us what we needed to know.

A thought occurred to me. "Did you happen to verify these weren't gargoyles or gorgon-based statues when you bought them?" I'd once worked a missing persons case where the victim was finally located as a statue in a cemetery after an unfortunate encounter with a gorgon. One of the few happy endings in my line of work.

"Naturally. I can show you the Certificate of Authenticity if you like."

"That's okay." It was a long shot anyway but still worth asking. "Would you mind if I had a moment alone out here? I do my best work uninterrupted." I tried that line with my kids many times over the years. Never worked. A Mad Hatter, however, was a different story.

He bowed. "Take as much time as you wish. I'd like this case solved quickly. As you can imagine, it's casting a shadow over the venue. I've had several parties cancel this week."

The Mad Hatter didn't seem to have any reason to want Dottie dead. She was good for business in every way and her death on the premises was anything but.

"Just out of curiosity, do you have any competitors in Savannah? Any business that would love to see you fail?"

He choked back laughter. "Are you suggesting one of my competitors may have murdered Dottie during a tea party in order to steal my clientele?"

I shrugged. "People have killed for less."

"No, absolutely not. There isn't another venue in town that's similar enough to this place to be considered direct competition."

I nodded. "Okay, it was just a thought."

I waited for him to retreat before directing my full attention to the statue. The broken neck was unsettling. The bloodstains had already been cleaned. I'd seen the initial report from Martin. I crouched down to study the base of the headless statue in case the team missed anything during their sweep.

"You won't find anything," a deep voice said. "They cleaned every speck. I was so impressed, I nearly offered them a job at my house and I'm very particular."

My gaze flicked to a tall man in a charcoal-colored suit and a crisp white shirt. No tie. The ends of his dark blond hair skimmed his collar.

My mysterious stalker.

"Nice trick with the roots, by the way," he remarked. "Subtle."

His smile revealed a set of fangs sharp enough to puncture an ice cube. It had been a long time since I'd seen a vampire. One of the byproducts of becoming a hermit.

"I asked Mr. Hatter for privacy while I conduct a survey of the crime scene."

"Yes, I couldn't help but overhear. A terrible tragedy, this whole affair." His voice reeked of education and privilege.

"Murders generally are."

He showed no sign of leaving, so I ignored him and continued my inspection of the courtyard.

As I bent over to examine the shrubbery for clues, I felt him looming over me. I glanced over my shoulder. "Do you mind?"

"Not at all. You're doing a grand job, I might add. Very thorough."

My glance became a glare. "You're mocking me."

"Not at all. I wouldn't dream of mocking an agent from Hex Support." He lowered his voice. "I heard you once used a vampire's own fangs against him."

I straightened and pivoted to face him. "You make me sound like the John Wick of the FBM."

He shrugged. "If the pencil fits."

I folded my arms and regarded him. "Who are you?"

"Someone equally invested in finding Ms. Neff's killer. With your skills and my resources, I think we can manage it in record time."

"And what resources are those?"

"That's on a need-to-know basis."

"I work alone, but thanks for the offer." I spun back toward the shrubbery.

He tapped me on the shoulder. "I wasn't suggesting you'd use my own fangs against me. We'd be on the same team."

I kept my focus on the shrubbery. "There's no team, Mr. Vampire. Now if you'll let me get back to work, I'd appreciate it—unless you're eager to see how I might use this shrubbery to persuade you."

There was a brief pause. "To be perfectly frank, I would very much like to see."

I twisted to look at him. "Do you have a death wish?"

He chuckled awkwardly. "Something like that. I can see you're not open to my suggestion at the moment. I'll get out of your way."

"Thank you."

I turned back to the shrubbery and my heart skipped a beat at the sight of a patch of blood. At least I thought it was until closer inspection revealed it was only a feather lodged between leaves. The bright red color matched Icarus's tail. No surprise if the bird was fond of playing Houdini.

I tucked the feather into my notebook and continued my search. By the time I finished, the natural light in the court-yard had dimmed. I'd done everything I could here. It was time to move on.

CHAPTER FIVE

There was no sign of dinner when I arrived at The Springhouse, so I decided to venture out on my own. I was too hungry to wait for Madam Lemonte. I wandered to Reynolds Square and my gaze landed on The Olde Pink House. The restaurant had an excellent reputation. Why not take a little time to indulge in good food and drink while I worked? As a Green Witch, I was as adept in the kitchen as I was in the garden, which made me the de facto chef of Dark Hollow. It was a rare treat for me to be fed by someone else.

The hour was early enough that the restaurant wasn't too busy. Once I was seated at a table, I immediately pulled out the envelope from Mandy and perused the guest list. There were handwritten notes next to each name. There were normal notes like 'vegetarian' and 'no alcohol.' There were also smiley faces and hearts. Those guests with favored status, presumably. Not too many of those.

I ordered a cocktail and moved on to the preliminary report from Martin. Based on the description of the fatal wound, the killer had an easier time removing Dottie's head than the statue's. Maybe they'd been in a full-blown rage by the time they attacked the statue or maybe the sharp blade was more suited to slicing through flesh than stone. Amazing that nobody heard the commotion. You would think the sound of a ruckus would've traveled from the courtyard. A blade through Dottie's neck might've been achieved quietly but not the toppling of a stone head.

I sipped my drink, thinking through what I'd learned so far. I had to get back in the habit of assessing the information in stages so as not to get overwhelmed. The last mystery I solved involved which animal from the sanctuary was stealing pillows from the house. Spoiler alert: it wasn't Gertie, the prime suspect. It was Edgar, Elizabeth's familiar. The albino raven had decided to impress Bella, the black swan, by building her a comfortable nest outside. Good thing we had an endless supply of coupons for Bed Bath & Beyond to cheaply replace the pillows.

As I tucked away my notes, my gaze snagged on the man at the neighboring table. "You've got to be kidding me," I said.

The vampire waved a hand and the metal of his wrist-watch caught the light. I had no doubt it was a Rolex.

"It seems a waste to take up two tables on such a busy night. Why don't I join you?"

Before I could respond that it wasn't remotely busy, he vacated his chair and seated himself across from me. I caught the whiff of an earthy scent. It wasn't cologne, but it was nice. If I weren't so irritated, I'd inhale more deeply.

"Who are you and why are you following me?" I demanded.

He unfolded his napkin with slow precision and placed it on his lap. "It takes a certain amount of hubris to think someone dining at this fine establishment must only be here because of you."

Embarrassment flooded my body and I prayed my face didn't betray me. "This can't be a coincidence."

"That we both chose the best restaurant in Savannah for dinner? No, I don't believe it is. It simply means we share excellent taste." His gaze traveled around the room. "This building is a survivor, like me." He cut a glance at me. "Like us. Do you know when it was built?"

"I'd guess late 1700s."

He nodded. "It survived the great fire in 1796 that destroyed hundreds of buildings in the city. A tragedy."

I drank more of my cocktail. "I'm sure your knowledge of local history will be far more interesting to the woman over there." I inclined my head to an attractive woman at a nearby table.

He didn't bother to turn and look. "There's only one woman I'm interested in sharing a table with tonight and I'm already seated across from her."

What a charmer. Fine, I'd play. Maybe he knew more about the case than he was letting on. "Why did you call me a survivor?"

"Ah, back to the topic of you again. I should've known."

My foot itched to kick him under the table.

I resisted the urge.

The server appeared at the table. Before I could say a word, the vampire ordered a Planter's Punch for me and a whiskey for him.

"On the rocks?" she asked.

He recoiled as though she'd suggested adding a cockroach garnish to his drink. "No, thank you. I prefer to taste the alcohol."

"I'll be back in a minute to take your dinner order." She hurried toward the bar.

I directed my attention back to the vampire. "For a

complete stranger and someone who claims not to be following me, you seem to think you know me."

He smiled and his blue eyes crinkled at the corners. "I'm no stalker, Ms. Fairfield. Only a professional admirer."

I slotted my fingers together on the table. "Let's start with that. How do you know my name?"

"In my line of work, I make it my business to know."

I leaned forward and fixed him with a hard stare. "And what exactly is your line of work?"

"The same as yours, except I'm in the private sector."

I straightened. "You're a PI?" He didn't strike me as a PI, or even an agent. He was too polished. Too refined.

"Consider me a consultant."

"And who do you consult?"

"Whom, Ms. Fairfield. I would think the mother of two Ivy League students would have a better grasp of grammar rules."

"Only one of the schools is Ivy League..." I began and then froze. "Wait. You know where my kids attend college?"

"Fraternal twins. Deacon James Watts and Imogen Katherine Watts. Eighteen years old. Deacon is a wizard who prefers math and science to magic and Imogen is a Book Witch like her aunt." He paused. "Elizabeth, is it?"

A lump formed in my throat. "Tell me again how you're not a stalker."

"I simply like to thoroughly research any prospective partners." Hesitation flickered in his eyes. "*Professional* partners."

"And how am I a prospective *professional* partner?"

"Because you've been assigned the Dottie Neff case and I think it would be wise if we worked together to solve it."

I couldn't resist a smile. "Oh, do you? And why is that?"

"Because I have been hired by a private party to do what they believe the FBM is incapable of doing." He opened his menu and started to peruse the items. "But having met you, I am of a different opinion." His brow lifted. "Oh, the filet comes with twice-baked potato. That clinches it." He closed the menu and smiled at me, displaying the hint of two sharp fangs. "What about you?"

I pretended to study the menu, although I'd already decided on the scallops. I was a sucker for seafood. "I'm surprised you don't already know."

"I prefer to be surprised on occasion." He paused. "But I would hasten to say the sea scallops."

My smug smile quickly faded, prompting a laugh from my companion.

"You have a remarkably poor poker face for an agent."

"I'm not in agent mode at the moment." I closed the menu with a snap. "I'm in don't-murder-the-annoying-vampire-mode."

He chuckled. "You wouldn't want to add any more work to your plate now, would you, Katherine? Or would you prefer I call you Kit?"

I stiffened. "You seem to have me at a disadvantage."

"Knowledge is power," he quipped.

The server returned to the table with our drinks and took our order that included the aforementioned entrees. Seeming to sense the tension between us, she removed my empty cocktail glass and beat a hasty retreat.

"Why don't you tell me your name since we're destined to be such good friends?"

"Palmer."

"Is that your first name or your last name?"

"Yes."

"Oh, I see. You're like Madonna and Cher but without the fashion sense."

"Those are outdated references, Ms. Fairfield. You might want to try Zendaya."

A vampire was telling *me* about outdated references? This was quite a day I was having.

"How old are you?" I asked.

"Does it matter?"

"Nope. Just being nosy. And I might be in the mood to tell an age joke later." I raised my glass and sipped. "Alcohol makes me funnier."

"No, alcohol makes you *think* you're funnier." He tasted the whiskey. "I'm old enough to know that your family's renowned estate was here before me."

Hmm. Dark Hollow was pretty old, so that didn't tell me much.

He raised an eyebrow when I drank half my punch in one gulp. "Are you planning to solve the case or hallucinate about it?"

"I don't get to indulge too often." I limited myself to an occasional glass of wine with dinner or cider with one of my sisters at our preferred watering hole.

"Not even now that your baby birds have flown the nest?"

"I still have two younger sisters at home."

He swirled the honey-colored liquid in his glass and drank. "Interesting to have such an age gap between you. Is it a witch thing?"

"And here I thought you knew everything." I took another sip of my cocktail and my head buzzed. I started to regret my choice of such a potent mixture.

"Elizabeth is...thirty-three?"

"Yes, and Grace is twenty-five, although she has a birthday coming up."

"And you're the glue that holds the family together."

I stared at him over the rim of my glass. "It stands to reason. I'm the oldest and the only mother."

"Must be lonely sometimes. All that responsibility."

"Sometimes, but I just take a walk in the sanctuary and

enjoy the company of the animals. That always makes me feel better."

I clamped my mouth shut. This wasn't like me at all. Why was I being so forthcoming with a complete stranger?

"You could be a vampire yourself, you know," he said. "You don't look like you've aged a day since you left Hex Support."

"Compliments won't get you far with me, Mr. Palmer."

"Just Palmer."

"Fine, Just Palmer. Why do you want to work together? Are you afraid I'll solve the case first and you don't want to be shown up by a woman?"

"I think you're a witch of remarkable talent, but you'd be fortunate to have me as an asset. It'll make you look better in that report you'll need to send to Martin if you can wrap this up quickly."

His inside knowledge of Hex Support was unnerving. The division was a secret, yet this vampire knew not only of its existence, but the names of its members.

I decided to be blunt. "Who's your insider at Hex Support?"

"What makes you think I have someone on the inside?"

"Because you can't possibly have access to this level of information without clearance or someone on the inside."

"I have access to other information you may not have in that little notebook of yours." He gestured to the notebook I'd tucked inside my handbag.

"Like what?"

"You might want to consider a trip to Jekyll Island."

"I thought no one lived on the island anymore. Isn't it a state park?"

"Ms. Fairfield, when have you known supernaturals to abandon a lap of luxury? If there's a way to remain hidden in plain sight, we'll find it. You should know as well as anyone."

That much was true. Dark Hollow shouldn't exist in the

human world, and yet it did. Fairfield witches had lived in the castle for centuries and had only raised a few eyebrows in the process. The building was almost a fairy tale in and of itself, grounded in reality yet somehow unbelievable.

"Does this suspect have a name?"

"Percival Mulgrew. It's a small island. I have no doubt you can root him out without much effort."

"If we're competing, why volunteer that? I'd think you'd prefer to watch me twist in the wind."

"I told you I'd rather join forces, but if we were to compete, I know I'd win."

"So you've already spoken to him?"

"No, but we could go together."

"Of course. Let's put a day and time on the calendar. Maybe we could have lunch afterward."

He rested his chin on the heel of his hand and gazed at me. "You're mocking me."

"I told you I work alone."

"You have the most mesmerizing eyes. I bet you used them to great advantage in your early days as an agent."

"I used whatever resources were available to me."

"Yes, one of the reasons you were their top agent, no doubt."

"James was better." The words tumbled from my lips and I blinked at the vampire in surprise. I'd never admitted that out loud before. I didn't want to acknowledge that he was the one who should've lived that day.

And that I should've died.

"If you don't mind me saying, all the reports suggest James was an excellent agent, but he didn't hold a candle to you."

"Thank you, but that simply isn't true." I pushed thoughts of my husband aside.

"Have you dated much since his death? It must've been terribly hard for you, especially in those early years."

"It was devastating. My whole world turned upside down in a single day." I curled my fingers around the base of the glass. "To answer your question, I haven't dated. It would take an incredibly special man to follow James, and to be blunt, and I don't think he exists."

Palmer's face went blank. "You're still young, at least by vampire standards. You have plenty of time to prove yourself wrong."

My stomach turned as my tongue recognized a familiar taste. I stared into the empty cocktail glass. "What did you put in my drink?"

"Nothing."

I glared at him. "I can feel it in my bloodstream. What is it?" I didn't know why I bothered to ask. I knew what it was.

He shifted in his chair. "I think you'll find the bartender added a lunaria seed to your punch." He cleared his throat. "At my request."

"What were you hoping to learn that you didn't already know?"

"I wanted to be certain that you and I could work together. And now I am." He raised his glass to mine. "Cheers to that."

I gaped at him. "You can't be serious. You just drugged me and yet you expect me to carry on with dinner and work with you? You're madder than the Mad Hatter."

"Why not? The food here is excellent and the company isn't so bad either."

I tossed my napkin on the table in a huff. "You're out of your mind if you think I'm going to sit across from you for another minute." I jerked open my handbag and pulled out my wallet.

He waved me off. "I'll cover the bill. I've seen what they pay you and it isn't enough."

I tossed a handful of bills on the table. "If you ever pull a stunt like that again, you'll find yourself bent over the nearest piece of furniture with your pants at your ankles."

He beamed. "I thought you were trying to discourage me?"

Okay, I needed to come up with a threat that wasn't designed for toddlers. Later—when I was clear-headed.

I stalked away from the table and through the dining room to the exit. The nerve of that guy. Imagine slipping a lunaria seed in the drink of a Green Witch and expecting her not to notice?

Halfway along the sidewalk, I stopped walking. The vampire clearly wasn't an idiot. What if he *did* expect me to notice? What if he was testing me?

My hands balled into fists. He *was* testing me. I was certain of it.

Sensing I was being watched, I looked back at the restaurant, but there was no sign of anyone.

I turned and continued the long walk back to my room.

CHAPTER SIX

I decided not to wait to pay a visit to Percival Mulgrew. Based on what I knew of Palmer so far, he wouldn't wait either. I wondered whether he really intended to follow me there, too.

I sent another text to Martin about Palmer. The last one had gone unanswered, which wasn't unusual for Martin, especially if another high-profile case landed on his desk.

Next I called Elizabeth from the corner of East Broad Street. My sister was excellent when it came to research.

She answered on the first ring. "Are you hurt? Is everything okay?"

"I'm fine," I assured her. "I could use your help with something." I explained where I was going and why I wanted an unconventional means of transport. "I checked the APIAS app, but I don't see a portal on the island."

"I don't know, Kit. This vampire sounds dangerous. Maybe you shouldn't go alone in case he follows you."

"I can handle myself."

"Give me five minutes. I'll check in the library."

I tapped my foot on the pavement while I waited. The

pleasant weather seemed to have drawn out every person in the city. A tour group passed by and I heard the guide talking about the various haunted locations. I'd yet to see a ghost since my arrival, although I felt their energy every so often. I'd once described it to Martin as a light pressure, like someone was pressing their thumb against the base of my skull. A strange sensation but one I'd learned to live with like white noise.

"I found something," Elizabeth said, sounding breathless. "Bonaventure Cemetery."

"Not the portal."

"No, there's a ferry that leaves from there, but you have to summon it."

"I see. Like crossing Styx. Do I need a special coin?"

"No. There's a specific headstone." She gave me detailed instructions.

"Thanks, you're the best."

"Anything else I can research? I have loads of time."

"Not right now. How's everyone?"

"Grace burnt dinner and Gertie chewed a hole in your favorite jacket, but otherwise good."

I closed my eyes and silently counted to ten. It was my fault for coddling them into adulthood. "I'll check in again soon."

"Take your time. We're fine here without you."

I wasn't convinced. I ended the call and ordered an Uber to take me to the cemetery.

"Need me to wait?" the driver asked.

I exited the car. "No, thanks. I'm meeting a friend."

His brow creased as he glanced at the cemetery. "To each their own, I guess."

Although the gates were closed, that didn't stop me from passing through. The cemetery was over 170 years old and over 100 acres. Marble carvings. Monuments. Live oaks. The pink azaleas were in full bloom. It was a beautiful spot despite the reminders of death all around me.

I wandered along the path and admired the headstones as I looked for the one I needed to approach.

Then I saw it.

The statue appeared deep in thought, her gaze fixed on nothing in particular. In her hand was a wreath. I approached the statue and placed both hands on the base.

I felt the warmth of the energy as it flowed from my fingertips to the stone, which glowed with an eerie blue light. The ground rumbled slightly and I took a few steps back to wait.

Bony fingers pushed their way to the surface, followed by an arm. Head and shoulders popped up next.

"Roundtrip to Jekyll Island, please."

The skeleton slid his legs from their earthly prison and produced a shrill whistle. A second skeleton climbed out of the dirt next to him.

Together they stumbled toward the river, occasionally banging their bones together. I got the impression they hadn't been called upon in quite some time and were out of practice.

An owl hooted in the distance, prompting a friendly wave from one of the skeletons.

When we reached the bank, the surface of the water bubbled. A rowboat rose from the depths. Seaweed clung to the sides and a fish took the opportunity to leap overboard back to the safety of the water.

The second skeleton climbed into the boat and took control of the oars. The first skeleton offered a bony hand and helped me into the boat.

A simple internet search revealed Percival's home address.

No need to waste time wandering aimlessly around an island. The night was cool and I wrapped my arms around me to stave off the chill. The moment we shoved off, a gust of air rushed past us that made my teeth chatter. The dampness of the boat didn't help matters.

I plucked a string of seaweed from the interior wall of the boat and closed my eyes. Seaweed held enough power for a basic warming spell. I sucked the residual energy from the plant and used it to heat up my body temperature.

Warmth flooded my body and I was able to relax and enjoy the remainder of the ride. The lights of Savannah grew faint and the stars shone brightly against a black shroud.

I was glad to have ditched Palmer. I didn't need the vampire tracking my every move. It was unsettling. Who did he think he was anyway? I didn't care whether he was hired by the President of the United States, I didn't owe him the fruits of my labor. This was my case and I was determined to solve it without help if for no other reason than to prove to myself I was still capable of doing the job. After that I'd be free to decide next steps. I was in my forties. My kids were in college now. I was still young enough and healthy enough to take advantage of my newfound freedom. How I intended to take advantage was still up for debate. I'd been debating all year, in fact, much to Grace's consternation. My youngest sister thought I was wasting away again in Dark Hollowville.

The boat continued south along the Intracoastal Waterway. Thanks to the wind, the vessel picked up speed and the skeletons increased the rate of their movements to coincide. Finally Jekyll Island loomed ahead. We approached Mile Marker 685 for the Jekyll Harbor Marina. I scanned the shadows for any sign of movement. All was quiet on the smallest of Georgia's Golden Isles barrier islands.

The first skeleton helped me to the dock and I noticed a huge piece of driftwood on the beach. Even under the cover of darkness, I could see the wood had been bleached by the sun. The knotty branches reminded me of the bones of my companions.

The historic district on the island had been dubbed the 'Millionaire's Village.' Wealthy families from the industrial age once spent entire summers on the island as part of the Jekyll Island Club. Their power and influence were felt across the nation. The Federal Reserve Bank was created here and the first coast-to-coast conference call happened here as well.

Thirty-four structures remained on what was once the grounds of the esteemed club. Pulitzers, Astors, Rockefellers, Goodyears, and Vanderbilts were members. It was Newport's forgotten cousin.

Dottie's cousin Percival had good taste in hideaways. I was curious to discover his story. Life on a small island suggested a reclusive nature, but not so reclusive that he avoided the tea party of the season.

I'd checked a map on my phone during the boat ride so I knew how to find Water Oak Way. Despite the late hour, soft light glowed in the downstairs window of the house.

Found you, Percival.

The historic house was well-preserved. Dark Hollow would've towered over it, of course, but that was true of most homes.

I stepped on the welcome mat and knocked. The sound echoed in the quiet night air. If anyone was awake within a mile radius, they would know someone was receiving a visitor.

The door swung open and a portly man stood in the doorway. Tufts of hair protruded above his ears and formed cloud-like patches on his head. His wire-rimmed glasses were too round for his face and they balanced on the edge of his nose, in danger of sliding to the floor. He didn't strike me as someone with the quick reflexes to catch them.

"Are you Percival Mulgrew?"

He squinted at me. "Yes. Can I help you?"

"My name is Agent Fairfield. I'd like to ask you a few questions about the death of your cousin."

"Death? That's putting it mildly."

"Yes, it is. Care to tell me what you know about it?"

He waved me in. "Would you like a drink? A brandy or I could boil the kettle for tea?"

"Any green tea?" It was late and I was drowsy from the cocktails. I could use the shot of caffeine. If I were home, I would've brewed a concoction of my own.

"I believe I do."

Percival guided me to a modest kitchen at the back of the house. The vinyl yellow chairs were in sharp contrast to the silky mauve chairs in Magnolia Hall. The metal legs of the chair squeaked as I sat.

"This must be an interesting place to live," I remarked. "So much history on one small island."

"Absolutely. Savanah is steeped in history, too, of course, but this was a playground for a lot of famous names. Some of the finest minds and richest bank accounts. They spent their summers here golfing and fishing until they finally abandoned their mansions and their beloved club."

"The Great Depression?"

He nodded. "The island didn't manage to bounce back until the state took control later on."

"It's like a resurrected ghost town."

"Of a sort. I like the peace and quiet. It's never very busy, not even during the height of the tourist season. I can take the bicycle path through the forest—see pine trees, live oaks, palmetto, magnolia—and end up on a beautiful beach without seeing another living soul."

Anonymity had its advantages.

"How about any dead ones?" I prompted.

"I don't have that particular ability, I'm afraid. My magic is too weak."

That was a handy segue. "Tell me about the tea party at The Mad Hatter."

"What makes you think I was there?" His gaze darted to the left. Anywhere was a better view than my face, apparently.

"You were seen there, Percival. Your costume wasn't quite the disguise you intended."

His head jerked back to me. "I had nothing to do with the murder. I keep my head down and mind my own business." He grimaced. "I shouldn't mention keeping my head down, should I? Seems insensitive."

"It was a long way to go for a party, wasn't it?"

He sputtered an incomprehensible response, then added, "Nobody turns down an invitation from the queen."

"Why were you invited?"

He seemed taken aback by the question. "I'm always invited. I'm a Mulgrew."

"What's the family connection?"

"First cousins on my mother's side."

I felt a low pressure building at the base of my skull. "How many of you will split the inheritance?"

His gaze flicked to a painting of wild ponies on the wall. "I don't know."

"Mr. Mulgrew, if you don't tell me, I'll find out from someone else. Let's make this easier on both of us."

He pursed his fat lips together. "There are seven of us."

"And you're certain you're all in the will? No one's been written out?"

His face slipped into shadow.

"Which one of you was written out?"

"Daisy."

"Why her?"

"Let's just say that Dottie had a low tolerance for imbeciles."

I pushed past the pressure. "In other words, Daisy doesn't qualify for Mensa?"

"She's a sweet, dopey girl with horrible judgment." Percival blew out a breath. "We've all tried to help Daisy over the years, but Dottie finally hit her limit and wrote her out of the will. She believed no amount of money could save Daisy from her own stupidity."

"That's harsh."

Percival pushed his glasses back to the bridge of his nose. "Dottie used to say Daisy's real father must've been a were-rooster."

"What caused the final straw?"

"That I don't know. Neither one talked about it, at least not to me. Knowing Dottie, it was something small and insignificant that rubbed her the wrong way like mismatched socks or a hat worn at a jaunty angle."

"She was that particular, huh?"

He wore a faint smile. "Sometimes."

"Can you give me examples of Daisy's questionable judgment?"

"Oh, let me think." He settled in the chair across from me. "She's flighty. One minute she's making birdhouses, the next she's blowing glass."

"She's a creative type." I scribbled the detail in my notebook.

"That's one description."

I glanced up at him. "And what do you do for a living?"

"I work from home." He pointed past my head. "My office is right through there."

"You're self-employed?"

"No, I'm a medical coder. My cousin Luke set me up with the job through a friend of his. The Wi-Fi is decent enough to let me work from home. I'm not much of a people person. I prefer my own company."

"Unlike Dottie," I commented.

He laughed. "Definitely not like Dottie. Her favorite place on the island was the most populated—the Clubhouse."

"It wasn't abandoned like the other buildings?"

"Oh, it was, but it's since been restored. If you want to socialize on Jekyll, that's the place to do it."

I rubbed the back of my head. "Any idea how old your house is, Mr. Mulgrew?"

"Yes, why?"

"Any chance of a ghost sharing it with you?"

"Not to my knowledge. Then again, I can't see them."

"No one moves your furniture around or opens and closes cabinet doors?"

He blinked at me from behind his glasses. "No."

I opted to change the subject. "Where can I find Daisy?"

"She wasn't there that night if that's what you're thinking. She wasn't invited to the party. Rufus offered to stay home with her to make her feel better, but she insisted that he go."

"Rufus is another cousin?"

He nodded. "Daisy's older brother."

"Not rumored to have a moron for a father, presumably."

He shook his head. "Rufus is happy-go-lucky, but far from stupid."

Kind, too, if he was willing to sit out the party of the season for his sister's sake.

"I'd still like to talk to Daisy." I looked at him expectantly.

"She lives on Seiler Avenue near Thomas Square."

"Are you the only one not living in Savannah then?"

Percival nodded. "As I said, I prefer the quiet."

"Before I go, if a tall man in an expensive suit shows up on your doorstep tomorrow, do yourself a favor and don't invite him in. He's been harassing people in the city and I have it on good authority he might travel to the island."

Percival raised his eyebrows. "Vampire?"

"Worse." I lowered my voice. "Jehovah's Witness."

CHAPTER SEVEN

Revolution was tucked down a cobblestoned side street. There was no sign to indicate its existence, only a metal door at the end of a short flight of stairs.

The interior of the speakeasy was like walking back in time. The roaring twenties theme was evident everywhere, from the wooden stools to the art deco prints on the wall.

A jazz quartet played in the corner. The music would make a conversation difficult, but I'd conducted interviews through noisier circumstances. I'd manage.

A hostess intercepted me. "You look lost, ma'am. Are you here for the Prohibition cocktail class?"

My gaze flicked to behind the bar where a blond woman was frantically mixing drinks.

"Jack Barnes is the instructor tonight, right?"

The hostess nodded. "He's the only one who teaches this class. That's why it's in such demand." She pointed to a door at the far end of the room. "Through that door and along the tunnel. It's the first door on your left."

"Thank you."

I threaded my way through the boozehounds. If I could

get to Jack before the class began, I could make a graceful exit and avoid the awkward moment when everyone realizes there's one more student than there should be.

One look at Jack Barnes and I understood his popularity. I'd hasten a guess that it had very little to do with the quality of the cocktails. With slicked-back hair, a trendy beard, and a physique that rivaled Dwayne 'the Rock' Johnson's, Jack looked like the sun at the center of the speakeasy universe. A small group was already assembled around him, which would make my plan for a quick interview mildly difficult.

"We've got room for one more," the bartender called out when he noticed me. "Are you Stella?"

"Afraid not."

"No worries. It's not my style to turn people away. I might need to see some ID, though. You've got to be twenty-one and over to participate." He winked.

"I've got two teenagers to prove it." I offered a friendly smile and took my place at the end of a long table.

"You? I find that very hard to believe."

Now I really understood the appeal of Jack Barnes. No wonder Dottie requested him for all her functions. I didn't blame her for desiring compliments from a man like Jack.

"Hold on. One more incoming. So sorry I'm late."

My jaw dropped open as Palmer strode into the room. He walked straight to my end of the table and looked at me expectantly.

"Scoot down," he said, flicking his fingers.

"I'm not scooting anywhere," I said in a harsh whisper. "This is my spot."

"I think we can squeeze in one more," Jack said. "If you could inch over a little bit."

Palmer shot me a triumphant look and I inched away from him.

"What are you doing here?" I hissed.

He maintained a neutral expression. "Same as you. Learning to make Prohibition cocktails." He held up the beveled glass for examination. "Of course some of us actually lived through the period and could make drinks like this in our sleep."

"Then I guess you don't need to be here. See you around."

"Oh, but I do enjoy a refresher every now and then. Keeps me on my toes."

The woman at the table next to us put a finger to her lips and shushed us.

"She seems to have mistaken this place for a library," he said under his breath.

"If everyone will consult the menu on the table in front of you, you'll see the list of ingredients for our first cocktail. French 75."

Palmer rubbed his hands together. "Oh, I love a good French 75."

"If you're a fan of gin, you'll love this drink."

A red-haired woman next to us raised her hand.

Jack snapped his fingers. "Remind me your name again. I keep calling you Ginger, but I know that isn't right."

The woman fluffed her hair. "My name is Marcia. I wouldn't object to you calling me Ginger, though."

"What's your question, Ginger?" Jack asked with an air of flirtatious charm.

"Is it a dry gin?"

"It can be, but we're going to experiment with a gin that has notes of cucumber and rose."

"And top it off with champagne?" Palmer asked. "That's the way I've always made it."

"I'll leave the addition of champagne up to the individual."

Palmer leaned over to me. "Champagne is what separates men from beasts."

I pretended to write in my notebook. "Beasts enjoy a good bubbly. Got it."

Once we mastered French 75, we moved on to an old-fashioned.

"Finally," Marcia's husband grumbled. "Something for the men."

"Before we start, does anybody need more bitters?" Jack asked.

Palmer gestured to me. "Oh, she won't be needing more of those. She has plenty to spare."

My hands balled into fists. It was going to take all my self-control not to punch him in that square jaw of his.

Jack walked us through the ingredients and measurements with his same charisma.

Palmer held up his finished product and admired it under the light. "Mine is perfect," the vampire declared.

I rolled my eyes. Of course it was.

He thrust the glass at me. "Taste it."

"After the last time? No thanks. I have no idea how you might've tampered with it."

"You watched me drink it. Here, I'll taste it again." He made a big show of slurping the liquid.

"Proves nothing. Maybe you developed an immunity to whatever you added to it."

His mouth twitched in amusement. "Are you making a Princess Bride reference?"

I averted my gaze. "I don't know what you mean."

"Aha! You are. I promise I have not added Iocane powder to your drink. The only ingredients are the ones our fearless teacher instructed us to add. Here, I'll prove it."

Before I could stop him, he turned to the couple next to us.

"Would you mind tasting this and telling me what you think?" he asked.

Marcia happily accepted. "I'm sure it's no worse than mine. I added too much club soda." She raised the glass to her lips and drank. "Oh my goodness, yours is delicious."

Palmer smoothed the front of his jacket. "Naturally."

Marcia handed the glass to her husband. "Darren, you have to taste this."

Her husband appeared less than thrilled by the prospect. I pictured him with a mug at home that declared in block letters—*no, you can't have a sip*. "I'll stick to mine, thanks."

"But honey, his tastes the way ours is supposed to."

Darren scowled.

Marcia took another sip before passing the glass back to Palmer. "Whatever you're doing, keep it up."

"Oh, I always do." He arched an eyebrow suggestively and I suppressed a groan.

I tasted mine again. I was a Green Witch, for crying out loud. My cocktail should taste better than a vampire's. Then again, he'd likely been mixing the drink since its inception and I rarely fixed cocktails. I'd been too busy raising the twins and parenting my younger sisters to enjoy a drink, although I could've used one more times than I cared to count.

"Don't take it to heart, Ms. Fairfield. You can't be good at everything." He paused. "I can, of course, but I'm a special case."

"You're a special case, alright," I grumbled.

He seemed to find my attitude amusing. "You're accustomed to being the best, aren't you? I know the feeling well."

"I haven't been the best at anything in quite a long time," I admitted.

His good-natured expression dissolved. "You still have much to offer. More than you realize."

"You know what would help?"

His eyebrows inched up. "Another drink?"

"If you stopped interfering with my case."

He huffed. "This is not your case. This is a case that was assigned to you by *your* organization, of which I am not affiliated."

"Exactly. You're not affiliated, so beat it."

"First you underestimate yourself. Now you're underestimating me."

"I'm not underestimating you. I'm simply telling you I work best unencumbered."

"I'm sorry you view me as an impediment. I consider myself an asset."

"Take off the last two letters and I agree with you."

He polished off the last of his drink. "You might as well finish yours. It might loosen you up before your conversation with our friend, Jack. Something tells me Jack likes loose women."

Raising my glass to my mouth, I narrowed my eyes at him. I'd never met anyone so infuriating. It was as though someone had hired him simply to make my return to Hex Support more difficult.

The class came to an end and I lingered at the table hoping for a quiet word with Jack. Unfortunately I had to wait for two female classmates to stop flirting with him before my turn. Palmer waited with me, despite my best efforts to shove him toward the door.

Jack finally made his way over to us. "Any questions about the recipes?"

"Not exactly. I'd like to speak to you about Dottie Neff."

His eyes grew wide. "Wow. I wasn't expecting that. I thought you might want to hire me." His eyes grew moist as he took a moment to compose himself. "What a terrible tragedy. I can't stop thinking about it. My doctor even tried to prescribe me Xanax, but I didn't want to go down that path. If I'm going to medicate, I'll stick to alcohol."

"We understand you were working the tea party," Palmer said.

I glared at him. "Do you mind? This is my interview."

"Oh, I assumed you two were together," Jack said.

"No, we've only just met," I said.

Jack seemed to mull that over. "Well, you two have great chemistry. Certainly more than Ginger and her husband."

I ignored the chemistry remark. "I'm told Dottie hired you for all her special occasions."

Jack's head bobbed. "I was her go-to. If I had a scheduling conflict, she'd pay me double to cancel."

"She was a woman who liked to get her way," Palmer noted.

"Most definitely. And she was very generous, so I didn't mind."

"It didn't hurt your relationships with other clients?" I asked.

"No, they understood that Dottie came first with me. They tried to time their events not to coincide with hers, but it happened on occasion."

"The Mad Hatter didn't mind that you displaced his own bartender?" I asked.

Jack waved a hand. "Nah. He's a good dude. A little strange, but aren't we all?"

I gave the vampire a long look. "Some of us more than others."

"Was your relationship with the victim strictly professional?" Palmer interrupted.

Jack seemed taken aback by the question. "Are you asking if I was knocking boots with Dottie Neff?"

"It isn't out of the realm of possibilities. Some men enjoy a romp with a cougar."

I bristled. "Please don't use that word."

The vampire flashed an innocent look. "What's wrong with romp?"

"I think she means cougar," Jack said.

Palmer cut me a glance. "Not a fan of big cats?"

"The term might be considered disparaging to women," Jack offered.

"Is it? I consider it a compliment." Palmer adjusted his tie.

"Can we focus on the important question?" I huffed.

"My relationship with Dottie was strictly professional, although I will admit to a mild flirtation. I knew she had a crush on me, but I never would've acted on it."

"Why not?" I prompted.

"It would only ruin a good thing. She hired me for all her events. Paid me extra. Built up my reputation. Why would I risk that by sleeping with her?"

Made sense. "You were a regular at her functions. What can you tell me about her family?"

Jack chortled. "You mean the Seven Dwarfs?"

Palmer frowned. "I thought the Mulgrews were magi."

Jack raked a hand through his hair. "That's my pet name for them."

Interesting choice.

"Did Dottie ever confide in you about them? Any arguments you can recall?"

Jack cleared away the empty glasses from the other students. "She was mean to one of the younger women. I don't know any of their names so I call her the dopey one. She seemed flighty, you know? She's actually the reason why I started calling them the Seven Dwarfs. Then I realized it fit, so the name stuck."

Jack's information seemed to correspond to what I'd been told by Percival.

"Do you mean Daisy?"

He snapped his fingers. "That's the one."

"Do you make up names for all your patrons?" I asked.

His expression turned sheepish. "I might."

Palmer puffed out his chest. "Really? What was my name when I walked in?"

Jack pointed to me. "Bambi." He swiveled to Palmer. "Gaston."

We exchanged confused looks.

The bartender rocked the shaker back and forth. "Bambi because you looked wide-eyed and innocent when you walked in here. That's why I teased you about your ID." His gaze flickered to Palmer. "Gaston because your vibe is like that dude from Beauty and the Beast who loves admiring himself in the mirror. No offense."

I stifled a laugh. I'd much rather be Bambi than Gaston.

"So if there are seven of them, there must be a happy one," I remarked. "Would you say it was Rufus?" Percival had used the term 'happy-go-lucky' to describe Daisy's older brother.

"Yeah, that dude is the life of the party. Always has a big smile for everybody, especially Dottie. You can tell she adores him." His smile faded. "Sorry, adored. Man, I can't believe she's gone. Who would do such a heinous thing? Mount her head on a statue like a psychopath. That part's true, right?"

"That part is true," I confirmed.

He winced. "Poor Dot. I know she had a reputation for being tough, but she was always so sweet to me."

"I bet," Palmer murmured.

"Anybody with a grudge? Any rivals outside of the family?"

He tugged his beard. "The only one I can think of is Polly Beaufort."

Palmer nodded. "I can see that."

I looked from one to the other. "See what? Who is she?"

"Another socialite," Palmer replied.

"Dottie complained about Polly scheduling events for the

same day just to compete with her," Jack added. "Polly even tried to hire me a few times, but I politely declined. Dottie wouldn't have liked it."

"It cost you money," I pointed out.

"Don't mind. Dottie was loyal to me so I was loyal to her. That's how I roll."

Another loyal employee. For someone with a difficult personality, she seemed to do well in that department.

"I even turned down the annual Spring Fling she's hosting tomorrow night," he continued. "One of those bloated formal affairs. Polly had originally scheduled it for the day of the tea party, but from the sound of it, Dottie asked her to reconsider."

I made a mental note. "Asked or threatened?"

"Don't know. You'd have to ask Polly about that."

"You'll need a dress," Palmer said to me. His gaze dropped to the floor. "And no sneakers. You're not a career woman in the Big Apple."

Jack snorted. "Polly likes a big crowd, but she's definitely particular about the guest list and the dress code. The big dude's right. If you want to get in, you'll need to dress to impress."

"I can help you with that," Palmer offered.

I locked eyes with the vampire. "I don't need your input on my wardrobe."

Palmer gave me an incredulous look. "Have you looked in a mirror today? Slap on some shoulder pads and a fanny pack and you're basically a walking homage to the Eighties."

Beaming, Jack slapped a hand on the table. "Holy smokes, you two. Like I said, chemistry."

CHAPTER EIGHT

Daisy Mulgrew's house was located on the east side of Savannah in the Live Oak neighborhood not far from Daffin Park. Residents were fortunate to have a variety of beautiful parks to visit. If I lived here, I'd make a point of rotating through each one and taking advantage of what Mother Nature had to offer. Of course if I lived here, I'd miss the gardens at Dark Hollow that I'd spent a lifetime cultivating.

The house itself was a Craftsman bungalow painted a pale sea-foam green with creamy-white accents and a deep front porch. The front porch was so inviting, I wouldn't object to conducting my interview right here. A rocking chair rested on the right side of the porch with a woven basket of yarn beside it. A potted plant sat to the left of the door. Fiddlehead. Its height and bright green leaves suggested a competent caretaker.

I knocked and the door opened with a squeak of the hinges. A petite young woman gazed at me with inquisitive eyes. Her brown hair was streaked with the kind of ash blond highlights that looked natural but could be courtesy of the salon. She wore a short-sleeved cotton dress that reached her knobby knees. Pink toenails peered back at me from her bare feet.

"Daisy Mulgrew?"

"That's right."

Before I could introduce myself, she ushered me inside. I crossed the threshold and immediately felt the warmth of the cozy decor. If a house could embrace you, this one was giving out bear hugs. The small house could've seemed cramped in the hands of someone with less skill. Daisy managed to keep it light and airy thanks to the selection of two off-white sofas separated by a glass coffee table and a white brick fireplace. A mix of light and dark blue accent pillows and a pale blue beach painting on the wall added a touch of serenity to the space. Daisy might be flighty, but she had excellent taste in home furnishings.

"Would you like a drink? I can make you a sweet tea or an Arnold Palmer. The tea's still brewing, but I can add a lot of ice to cool it down faster."

"I'm fine, thanks." Sugar went straight to my middle, much like everything else I ate and drank these days. I sensed menopause on the horizon the way cows sensed impending rain. I opted to ignore it—most of the time. No point in whining about things beyond my control.

"Do you need help carrying the clay?" she asked. "I think I ordered fifty pounds so I bet it's heavy."

I squinted at her. "Clay?"

"Aren't you here with my clay delivery?"

"No, I'm sorry."

"That's okay. Have a seat," Daisy offered. Her friendly nature suggested we were old acquaintances. I got the impression she was like this with everyone. She probably invited the mail carrier in for cupcakes.

"What's the clay for?" I asked.

I chose the sofa that faced the rest of the house for a

better view of the interior. The footage couldn't be an inch over a thousand square-feet. From my vantage point, the dining room and kitchen appeared as impeccable as the living room.

"Oh, a new art project. I'm obsessed with pottery at the moment." Daisy sat on the sofa opposite me and tucked her legs underneath her.

"I saw a basket of yarn on the porch."

She waved a dismissive hand. "Last month's creative project. I made a scarf, but I found the repetition boring, so I've sort of given up on it. You're welcome to take the yarn if you're interested."

It occurred to me that Daisy would hate my life. The last decade had been a routine that revolved around the twins, my sisters, sanctuary animals, and Dark Hollow. There was no switching up the schedule on a whim. There were priorities and my hopes and dreams weren't among them.

Daisy gave me a sly look. "Aren't you going to ask me about Dottie?"

"What makes you say that?"

"You're a cop, aren't you?"

Not as dopey as I was led to believe. "Do I look like a cop?"

"No, but you have a serious face and sensible shoes."

"I do have a serious face, don't I? My children used to call me Serious Black, like the Harry Potter character except spelled..." Daisy looked at me with a blank expression. "Never mind. I'm Agent Katherine Fairfield and I'm with the Federal Bureau of Magic."

She shifted her feet to the floor and wiggled her toes. "Why a federal agent? Dottie was a local."

"In certain cases, they like to bring in a specialist."

Her brow furrowed. "If you're the specialist, then who's

the man I spoke to earlier? He wasn't a cop either. His suit was too expensive."

"You didn't ask?"

"To be honest, he was so good-looking, I didn't bother. I invited him in for a drink, same as you, but I think I stared at him with my mouth open most of the time he was here." Her giggle quickly morphed into a snort. It was surprisingly charming. "He had the most gorgeous eyes."

"By any chance, was this man a vampire?"

She straightened in her seat. "As a matter of fact, yes. I can't believe I don't remember his name. It isn't every day I invite someone that handsome into my home."

"What kinds of questions did he ask you?"

"The same ones you're about to ask, I guess. Why wasn't I at the party? What are my feelings about Dottie's death? Why did she cut me out of her life?"

"And what did you tell him?"

She plucked at the hem of her dress. "That Dottie was a short-tempered, mean-spirited woman with the patience of a racehorse and she disliked me because I am the exact opposite."

Very insightful for an imbecile. I was beginning to think everyone had misjudged her.

"Do you have an alibi for the time of the tea party?"

Her head bobbed. "I was at the Clay Spot for a pottery class. You can confirm with the owner."

I wrote the information in my notebook. "Was there a specific incident that led to the estrangement?"

Daisy reached for a light blue pillow and hugged it to her chest. "It had been brewing for quite some time. She insulted me at her birthday party last year, called me a flake and a moron, and the family refused to put up with it. They took their gifts and went home. She wrote me out of the will after that, or so I was told." She shrugged. "I've never shared her desire to show off or her interest in money anyway. Dottie called me 'simple' but really it's my life that's simple and I prefer it this way. Money and magic only complicate matters."

A simple life seemed to suit her. "Did you have any contact with Dottie after the dust-up?"

Daisy pressed her lips together. "She came to my brother's birthday party, although I didn't expect her to miss it. She adored Rufus. I would've been happy to speak to her, but she stayed at the opposite end of the room the whole evening. When I tried to approach her, she used magic to keep me at bay."

"What kind of spell?"

"Invisible wall. I bumped my toe twice trying to reach her and finally gave up. She laughed, of course. She always found her magical pranks so funny. I thought they were terrible and showed a lack of compassion and empathy."

"What about the rest of your family? Did anyone intervene when she manifested the invisible wall?"

"Rufus politely asked her to stop. He tread carefully with her, but she was generally willing to listen to him."

"Why would she listen to him?"

Daisy bubbled with laughter. "Percival thinks it's because Rufus is technically the oldest cousin except he was born out of wedlock, but I think it's his nature. Rufus is a happy guy and people hate to be the reason his smile turns upside-down. Works on me, too. I was upset about my doves a few weeks ago and Rufus dropped everything to come by and cheer me up."

I was almost afraid to ask. "What happened to your doves?"

"Oh, I was in a magic phase—like a magician not a mage. I'd ordered a bunch of doves for one of my acts, but I accidentally left the cage unlocked when I was practicing outside and they all flew away." She smacked her forehead. "It was a disaster."

I was beginning to grasp Dottie's frustration. The victim appeared to like things a certain way. The pranks were only funny if she did them. The magic was scheduled in advance. Daisy was a wild card. An accidental disruptor.

"Tell me about the rest of the cousins," I said.

"You should come tomorrow and meet them for yourself."

I frowned. "Come where?"

"To the reading of the will. We'll all be under one roof. It'll make your job easier, won't it?"

"You said she wrote you out of the will."

Daisy crossed her ankles. "I'm still going. The whole Mulgrew side of the family will be there and I'm a Mulgrew. If Dottie manages to erect an invisible wall to lock me out, I'll be more impressed than annoyed."

"Did you happen to mention the reading of the will to the handsome vampire?"

"No, I don't think it came up."

Good. The outcome of the will might give me the information I needed to crack the case and return to Dark Hollow in time for...Well, in time for nothing in particular. Still, if one of the twins arrived home unexpectedly, I'd hate to not be there. I'd been present for every crisis from mean girls at school to losing competitions to the worst crisis of all—losing their father. I wasn't about to ruin my perfect streak of availability.

"Just so you know, the vampire isn't a cop or an agent," I told her. "If he stops by again, I'd advise not answering the door."

A look of alarm crossed her delicate features. "Is he dangerous?"

"I haven't decided," I said truthfully. "But he's muddying the waters of the investigation."

"But he's so good-looking. Telling me he's dangerous only makes him more appealing, although he's probably too old for me." She cocked her head. "You're single. If he ends up not being dangerous, you should go out with him."

"How do you know I'm single?" I was more curious than annoyed by the assumption.

"I already told you. Serious face. Sensible shoes."

I glanced down at my New Balance sneakers. "Those could also be the markers of someone married to the same person for a long time."

"True, but you're not wearing a ring and there's no sign of indentation on your skin so if you're married, it's not a recent separation."

My eyebrows lifted. "That's very perceptive."

Daisy smiled. "I've always had good observational skills. Everyone assumes the opposite when they view you as flaky and inconsequential." Her smile faded as though she remembered something.

"What is it?" I prompted.

"Nothing." She bit her lip. "I just remembered something."

"Something to do with Dottie?"

She nodded. "I thought I saw Dottie after she died."

"Where?"

"Here in my house." She hugged herself. "For a split second I thought she'd come to prank me even in death. It would be so like her."

"Why do you think it wasn't her?"

"Because no one else has seen her and I'm basically the weakest one of us, magically speaking. It was such a fleeting glance..." Her brow furrowed. "Besides, I'd be the last person she'd want to see anyway." She relaxed her arms. "It was my imagination hard at work. Guilt has a way of making you see and feel things."

"Guilt?" I queried.

"Not guilt over killing her, of course. I would never hurt anyone. More that she's dead and we left things on bad terms."

"It wasn't your fault, though."

"I know, but it doesn't stop me from feeling the way I feel."

Daisy's mind was far more complex than Dottie gave her credit for.

"The guilt will fade in time," I told her. "I know it doesn't seem that way when you're in the thick of it, but time has a way of softening life's sharp edges."

Daisy met my sympathetic gaze. "You sound like someone with firsthand experience."

"You live long enough and it's inevitable, unfortunately."

She smiled. "You say that like you're ninety years old."

I put away my notebook. "Sometimes I feel ninety."

"You should try sticking your hands in clay. It sounds strange, but it's very soothing."

"I was thinking more along the lines of a dove delivery to liven things up."

She laughed. "Mistakes are what make us interesting, Agent Fairfield. If we were all perfect, life would get boring pretty quickly."

CHAPTER NINE

I left Daisy's feeling confident the younger mage had nothing to do with Dottie's death. I confirmed her alibi for the time of the tea party and moved on to the next priority—a formal dress for Polly Beaufort's Spring Fling. I wasn't about to spend money on a new dress. It made sense to portal home and grab one from my closet. It would also give me a chance to do a little research on my adversary—and I didn't mean Dottie's killer.

I opened the app to find the nearest portal. There was a convergence of ley lines not far from The Olde Pink House. It figured. Maybe Palmer would show up and try to hitch a ride home with me.

I followed the app to the precise spot and felt vibrations emanating from a giant live oak. The roots were probably soaking up all sorts of magical energy from the ley lines. Cutting a glance over my shoulder, I made sure no one was watching me. I pressed both hands on the tree trunk and formed a connection with the portal.

"Dark Hollow," I said.

The vibrations spread from my vocal cords to my chest.

The tree bark dissipated, revealing a familiar hall. I stepped forward and entered the portal.

I located my sisters in the kitchen. The room was so large and airy that light streamed in from multiple window sources. At Dark Hollow, the kitchen truly was the heart of the home, which suited me well as a Green Witch.

Grace glanced up from the mess she was currently making on the counter. Her hair was wild and her face was dusted with flour. "You're back." She didn't sound thrilled.

"Just in time to save the kitchen from your creative process, I see." I inclined my head toward the fine layer of flour on the counter.

"It's an experiment," Grace said. "I'd like to see if I can reverse bake."

I looked at Elizabeth seated on a stool at the counter. "Do I even want to know?"

Elizabeth shrugged. "It's interesting, but messy."

"I'm using magic to change the cookies back to their original ingredients. Reverse baking."

"Why would you want to do that?"

Grace spread her arms wide. "To see if I can. Why else?"

I gave Elizabeth a sharp look. "Did you even attempt to stop her?"

"Not when there are cookies involved. I'm not a monster." She paused. "More like a cookie monster."

"Priorities," I remarked.

"Did you solve the case?" Elizabeth asked.

"Not yet."

"Then why are you here?" Grace demanded.

"To make sure you don't douse the place in sugar and flour, obviously."

Grace sniffed. "You didn't object when I was conducting these types of experiments with Imogen and Deacon."

"That was different," I said. "Children should experience that kind of fun. You're twenty-five."

"Twenty-six at the end of the week," Elizabeth pointed out.

Grace's pale eyebrows drew together. "And I'll still be a Chaos Witch when I'm eighty-five. What's your point?"

I shot a glance at Elizabeth for support. She and I were the practical ones of our trio. I knew she'd understand my position.

To my surprise, Elizabeth sided with Grace. "Grace is right. This is who she is and who she wants to be. Who are we to set her limits?"

I felt deflated. "Carry on then, but I'm not on the cleaning committee."

"Dark Hollow will take care of itself," Grace said. She wiped her hands on her striped shirt. No surprise she didn't bother to wear an apron.

"We don't use house magic to clean up our own messes," I admonished her.

"If you haven't solved the case, why are you home?" Elizabeth asked.

"I need a dress."

Grace cracked a smile. "Liar. You were homesick."

"Maybe a little," I admitted. I sat on the stool next to Elizabeth and avoided touching the flour-covered counter. "But I do need a dress."

"I can't help with that," Elizabeth said. "My dresses are all too long for you."

"No, but you can help me with more research."

Elizabeth swiveled toward me. "I'm listening."

"Ever hear of a vampire named Palmer? He's young enough to look mid-forties. Dark blond hair. Six-four. Very wealthy."

"Is Palmer his first name or last name?" Grace asked.

I shrugged. "Both?"

"Cool, like Zendaya," Grace said.

Annoyance bubbled to the surface as I remembered Palmer's jibe. "Yes."

"Never heard of him," Grace said. "Is he on social media?"

It hadn't occurred to me to check. "I don't know."

Grace pulled her phone from her pocket and tapped the screen. "Palmer is a common name, but I don't see anybody that matches your description."

"I don't recognize the name either, but you might want to ask the ancestors," Elizabeth suggested. "If he's a vampire, they might know him."

I glanced in the direction of the spiral wooden staircase where the portraits of our witchy ancestors resided on the wall. I chatted with most of them on a semi-regular basis, except Anastasia. We all avoided Anastasia.

"I'll ask Aunt Elodie." She was the biggest gossip and, thus, the most likely to have dirt on a mysterious vampire.

"Ooh, he's cute," Grace said. She turned the phone so we could see the screen.

"He's too old for you," I said.

Grace looked at the screen, frowning. "How can you tell?"

"His bio is right under his name."

Grace laughed. "I didn't notice the fine print. I was too focused on the abs."

Elizabeth snorted. "It's a good thing you spend most of your time here. I'd hate to see you on a dating app."

"My nightmare," I agreed. It was enough to worry about my own children out in the world.

"I made it through college unscathed," Grace argued.

"Because we sent you to an all-female college," I pointed out.

"And you wouldn't believe the number of girls who had crushes on me."

"Oh, I believe it. What does his bio say?" I scanned the small print. "Entrepreneur. Very detailed."

"That usually means unemployed on dating sites," Grace said.

"He's employed," I said. "I'm just not sure by whom. Let me have a word with Aunt Elodie. When I come back, I wouldn't object to a snack. Portals make me hungry."

Round and round I went as I climbed the staircase, fixing my hair along the way. Aunt Elodie liked when we made an effort with our appearance. I wasn't about to put on lipstick, but I didn't object to untangling my hair.

My hand gripped the smooth wood of the banister as I climbed. To the untrained eye, the floating staircase was an architectural marvel. I was aware of a similar structure in Charleston, South Carolina at the Nathaniel Russell House. The house had been built by a wealthy shipping merchant in 1808 and was now a museum. The Russell House staircase, however, was an inventive construction of cantilevered steps. Dark Hollow's staircase was simply the product of magic.

I halted at Aunt Elodie's portrait. She looked like Angelica Huston, only with stark white hair instead of black. Her lips were ruby red and her eyes were two dark pools that threatened to claim you if you stared at them too long. Despite her arresting appearance, she had the lovable nature of a puppy and a propensity for gossip that continued after her death.

I touched the picture frame with one hand and formed a connection with the portrait. "Aunt Elodie?"

"Where have you been, young lady? It's been so long, I honestly can't remember the last time I spoke to you."

"It was two weeks ago."

"And what took you so long to come back? It isn't like you're busy now."

"I'm working on a case this week."

Her mouth formed an 'o' shape. "You don't say." She leaned forward out of the portrait. "Did you hear that, witches? Our Kit is back at work. Isn't it wonderful news?"

"It's only one case. I owe Martin a favor."

My aunt made a face. "You owe Martin a favor? Don't be absurd. If you ask me, that entire organization owes you a debt of gratitude."

"I'm not here to talk about the past, Aunt Elodie."

She gave me an appraising look. "Then why are you here?"

"I'd like to know about a vampire called Palmer."

A sly smile took hold of her ruby red lips. "Palmer, eh? Where'd you come across such a fine specimen?"

"Savannah. He's been hired privately to work the same case. It seems the FBM isn't held in high esteem by his client. They want to make sure the job is done right." Or something to that effect.

She sniffed. "Well, they clearly didn't realize Kit Fairfield would be assigned the case then. There's no one better, if you ask me."

I smiled. I could always count on the ancestors to boost my confidence. When I was younger, every basic act was met with a burst of rousing applause. They celebrated each and every accomplishment, however minor, and made me feel like the most special witch on the planet. It was only later that I realized I wasn't worthy of their accolades.

"What does Martin say about him?"

"Nothing. He's been too busy to answer my questions."

"Typical man. Throw you into the deep end after thirty years and let you drown."

"Ten years, Aunt Elodie."

She blew a raspberry. "Who can keep track? Ten...thirty. It's all the same after a while."

"Can you tell me anything specific about Palmer?"

"Other than he's devastatingly handsome and knows it,

no. Buckets of money, too, although I feel like that's a given. If you're a vampire with no money, your immortal life has taken an unfortunate turn and you should just stake yourself."

"Aunt Elodie, that's a terrible thing to say."

"Oh, please. Think about it. If you've had a century to figure out how to accumulate wealth and still haven't managed it, turn in your fangs."

I laughed. "Thanks for your help."

"You should ask Anastasia. She's more likely to keep tabs on vampires."

I cut a glance in the direction of Anastasia's portrait. I wasn't in the mood for the older witch. "Maybe later. I need to find a dress for a formal party."

Aunt Elodie clapped. "That sounds fun. Oh, I'm jealous now. Wear the dark blue dress that pushes up your bosom."

I cringed. I was forty-four and still hated the word 'bosom.' "I don't need to look good for this party."

She booped my nose. "Oh, sweetie. I don't care if you're going to the dentist. Your bosom should always look good."

"Always a pleasure, Aunt Elodie."

"Don't be a stranger," she called after me.

I returned downstairs and plucked my handbag from the counter.

"Do you need the car?" Elizabeth asked. "I was planning to run a few errands this afternoon."

"No, you take it. I'm using the portal."

"Back to Savannah?"

"Not yet." I lowered my voice. "I realized I haven't bought anything for Grace's birthday. I'll do it now before I go back to Savannah." It wasn't like me to miss milestones. One assignment with Hex Support and I was already falling behind in my personal life.

Elizabeth's brow lifted. "You're in the midst of a murder investigation. I don't think you need to worry about a birthday present. Grace is going to be twenty-six, not ten."

"I haven't missed giving her a birthday present and I'm not about to start now." Even during the four years I attended college, I managed to send a gift to celebrate my sisters' birthdays. After our mother died, it seemed even more important to prioritize family occasions.

I hurried through the house, hoping I didn't cross paths with Grace along the way. If she knew I was headed to Guilty Treasures, she'd know the reason.

"Where are you off to in such a hurry?" Grace asked.

Too late.

I swallowed hard. "Research for the case."

"Savannah?"

"No, Guilty Treasures." I was a terrible liar.

She brightened. "Ooh, can I come? I wouldn't mind looking at the pretty trinkets while you attend to business."

"Sorry, you can't. This case is high-profile, remember? Completely confidential."

Her brow furrowed. "But you've asked for help with other bits and pieces. Why is this different?"

I brushed past her, my heart racing. "Because it is. I'll see you for dinner." I'd squeeze in a meal with them before I returned to Savannah for Polly's party.

"Cool," she called after me. "What are we having?"

"Ask Elizabeth," I yelled over my shoulder.

I quickened my step to get to the portrait in case Grace decided to follow me anyway.

The pastoral image changed to a shop interior. The style was Rockwell in a darker palette. I stepped forward and entered the shop.

Ezra Potts was the proud owner of Guilty Treasures. I wasn't sure how long he'd been in business, only that the shop opened before I was born. He knew most members of my family and was a valuable resource for magical objects, as well as the person we came to when items in Dark Hollow went haywire. Just because an object was enchanted didn't mean it didn't require fixing.

The shop was the kind of messy, dusty interior that one associated with secondhand bookstores or the attic of an elderly relative. Ezra believed that the untidy atmosphere was the best way to showcase his wares. I wasn't convinced, and always arrived armed with a packet of tissues for the inevitable fit of sneezes I'd endure.

On my way to the counter, I paused to admire a golden lamp on a shelf. The metal was dented and had lost its shine, but I could see its potential.

"In the market for a genie?"

I turned to smile at the shopkeeper. "Good afternoon, Ezra."

He looked exactly the same as the last time I'd seen him. From the neck up, he resembled an absent-minded professor. Tufts of gray hair sprouted from his head in no particular pattern and he sported a pair of wire-rimmed glasses that had a habit of sliding down his nose. From the neck down was another story. He wore a black Bon Jovi T-shirt and faded black jeans. If he stepped out from behind the counter, I had no doubt he'd be wearing a pair of black biker boots or Gucci slides, depending on his mood.

"Haven't seen you since last summer when you were here for the twins. I thought you might be in mourning over the empty nest."

I abandoned the lamp and approached the counter. "I've been trying to adapt to the new normal."

"How did they like the antique maps for their dorm rooms? Big hit, I hope."

"The perfect choice."

He pushed his glasses to the bridge of his nose. "I thought as much. I suppose it's almost time for their summer break."

"Soon, although I don't expect them in time for Grace's birthday, which brings me to the reason for my visit. I'm on a mission to find the perfect gift for my sister."

"That should be simple enough. As I recall, she's easy to please."

"She definitely likes shiny objects, regardless of their use or value."

He smiled. "Sounds like the ideal customer to me."

I drummed my fingers on the countertop. "Anything new in stock?"

"Always. Are you thinking form or function?"

"Either. I'm willing to spend a little extra out of guilt."

He pointed to a display case behind me. "There is a lovely pocket watch in there that came from the estate of a recently-deceased fairy. It's collected a lot of dust over the years."

The average person would assume he meant actual dust, but I knew better. "What kind of magic?"

"This fairy family specialized in beauty. I haven't had the chance to fully experiment on the watch yet, but so far it has the kind of filters that people love to play with on their phones."

"Grace might enjoy that." I pondered the pocket watch. "Does it have a filter for animal faces? She's loves those."

"I haven't seen animals. So far I've seen glitter and anti-aging."

"I'd give her another twenty years before she cares about an anti-aging filter." I continued to search the shop.

"What about something for her familiar? A bejeweled collar?"

I grimaced. "That would last about five seconds before it got torn to shreds."

"Fair enough."

I turned my gaze to the display case behind him. "You've got new items behind the safety glass. Anything Grace could handle?" Ezra kept certain pieces behind a magical wall, usually enchanted objects that would wreak havoc if left out in the open.

He swiveled to regard the contents of the case. "Nothing springs to mind. The moonstone is pretty, but not something Grace would find useful."

"It seems pretty basic. Why is it behind safety glass?"

He smiled. "Ah, because this is no ordinary moonstone." He tapped the glass. "If I were to place this stone between us, it would magnify your power."

"No thanks. Fairfield witches have more than their share as it is."

He smirked. "I thought as much."

"I hope you're not selling amplifiers to people who might abuse their power."

"Oh, no. I'm very selective with my customers, as you know." He gazed at the bluish stone on the shelf. "To be fair, this one is fairly weak and wouldn't do much harm, but my policy is to disable amplifiers while in my shop. Nobody wants to end up like poor Roy Hoskins."

"What happened to him?"

"Left all his amplifiers enabled. One day a powerful wizard walked through the door and blew up the shop. Took half the block with it." Shaking his head, he clucked his tongue.

I examined the moonstone. "Why is this one weak?"

"The previous owner made it for himself. It's infused with his specific type of magic. You're a Fairfield; you know how it works."

I did. Although I was a Green Witch, the magic that flowed through my veins was the same as the magic that flowed through my sisters. Our inherited magic manifested in each of us differently based on our individual characteristics, similar to the expression of DNA.

"When the owner died," Ezra continued, "his hold on the stone ended and the amplifier became a free agent, so to speak."

I examined the moonstone from across the counter. "So it would amplify my power, but it works best if I had the same magic as the original owner?"

"Precisely."

"Yeah, I don't think Grace needs an amplified moonstone for her birthday, however weak. Her chaos magic is strong enough."

"I might have a few items in rose quartz."

I chuckled. "She grew out of that phase years ago."

"Still, she might enjoy it for sentimental reasons."

I felt myself relenting. "Might as well look."

"I have a few contenders." Ezra rounded the corner of the counter. "Follow me."

I glanced down at his footwear and was disappointed to see a pair of black rhinestone sneakers sparkling at me. I didn't even guess those as an option. How did I expect to solve a murder mystery when I couldn't even identify the shoes of someone I'd known for over four decades?

Ezra guided me to a set of shelves in the middle of the shop. They were lined with jewelry boxes.

"Are any of these charmed?"

He smiled. "Would I sell them if they weren't?"

I noticed a necklace with a simple blue stone. "What about that one?"

"Seems a bit subtle for Grace."

"It's for me." It matched the dark blue dress I was planning to wear tonight and it had been ages since I'd bought myself jewelry for no reason.

Ezra's eyebrows danced with surprise. "It's perfect for you,

Kit, although you don't need the enchantment." He removed the necklace from the shelf and clasped it around my neck. "It makes you more agreeable to everyone you meet."

The ideal accessory to wear to Polly's party. "I'll take it."

"And for Grace?"

An idea clicked into place. "Do you have any kitchen items?"

"Kitchen? Isn't that your domain?"

"I'm trying to loosen my grip. She's an adult and I don't do her any favors by creating an invisible wall around my so-called areas."

He clapped my shoulder. "Well said, Kit. I think I have just the thing."

CHAPTER TEN

I stood in line on the wraparound porch and waited my turn for admission to the Spring Fling. The house was grand by Savannah standards, although Dark Hollow tended to dwarf even the most lavish human house. It had been quite some time since I had to make myself presentable for a formal party. I was grateful to have two younger sisters with more fashion sense. Well, one sister. Elizabeth knew a lot about fashion if it was part of a chapter in a history book. Same with furniture. She could spot a Louis XVI wingback from twenty yards, but she got a blank look whenever someone mentioned IKEA. Grace was able to select a pair of tasteful black pumps that complemented the dress.

"Katherine Fairfield," I told the bouncer once it was my turn.

He scanned his phone. "I'm afraid you're not on the list, Ms. Fairfield."

I focused on the blue stone around my neck. "If you'd check again, I'm certain..."

The bouncer gazed into my eyes. "I'm deeply sorry. I want

more than anything to see your name on that list, but I don't."

"That's because Ms. Fairfield is my plus one," a deep voice said. A deep, familiar voice that sent chills down my spine.

I turned to look up at him and wasn't the least bit surprised to see the smirk on his face.

The bouncer's head bobbed. "Of course, sir. I'll add her next to your name. No trouble at all." He waved us inside.

My 'date' snaked a hand along my waist and escorted me across the threshold. I resisted the urge to smack his hand away. Wouldn't want to risk expulsion now that I was inside.

"You look stunning, Ms. Fairfield. I didn't expect you to part with your sneakers. I was sure I'd glimpse white rubber soles poking out from beneath the hem of your dress."

"I can run just as fast in these shoes." Which, truthfully, wasn't very fast at all.

He leaned down and brushed his lips against my ear. "See? I have my uses after all. Work with me. I promise I make a wonderful teammate. I can be very persuasive."

I smiled at him through gritted teeth. "Not a chance." I broke away and mingled in the crowd in search of my suspect.

Polly Beaufort made no bones about giving me the once-over. The tilt of her head was slow and deliberate. "Apologies, sweetness, but I don't believe I know you."

"I do."

I turned at the sound of a smooth and smoky voice. "Anthony?"

The older vampire smiled, displaying a set of perfect fangs. Veneers, in fact, because the last time I'd seen him, I'd broken six of his teeth including the primary fangs.

He clasped my hand and brought it to his thin lips. "Katherine Fairfield. To what do we owe the pleasure?"

Polly gave me an appraising look. "A Fairfield witch in my home? It's an honor." She bowed her head slightly.

Anthony kept his eyes locked on mine as he released my hand. "No hard feelings about our last meeting, in case you're wondering."

"All in the line of duty," I said.

Polly didn't bother to contain her interest. "I sense a story there. I'd love to hear about it over a glass of port later."

"I'm afraid I won't be staying long," I told her. "I'm only here for information."

Anthony's thick eyebrows inched up. "Back at work, are we? I thought I heard you retired."

"I did. This is a favor. One and done."

"For Martin?"

"I'd rather ask the questions, if you don't mind." I pivoted to Polly. "I'm investigating the murder of Dottie Neff."

Polly sucked in a breath. "A dreadful affair. I still can't believe she's gone."

"Come now, Polly. You can't pretend to be mourning her," Anthony said.

Polly seemed affronted. "I absolutely mourn her passing. She was one of the few Savannah supers I respected." Her narrowed eyes focused on me. "I suppose that's why you're here. Everybody knows I was her nemesis."

An interesting assessment. "You were hers, but she wasn't yours?"

Polly offered a delicate shrug. "Such rivalries are beneath me."

"Did you attend the tea party?" I asked.

Polly made a dismissive noise. "Certainly not."

"Where were you that day?"

Polly batted her exceptionally long eyelashes. "Which day was it again? I'm afraid I don't keep track of other people's social calendars. My own is quite enough."

"The sixteenth," Anthony interjected.

Polly nodded. "I was in a tennis tournament at the club.

There were dozens of people in attendance. You can confirm my story with any one of them, although I ask that you use discretion. I'd rather not have the gossip flag hiked up to full mast."

Even if I confirmed her story, it didn't rule her out. Someone like Polly Beaufort hired people to do her bidding. She'd be unlikely to get her own hands dirty.

"Are we finished?" Polly asked with a withering glance. "I'd like to mingle with my invited guests." She made sure to emphasize the word 'invited.'

"Thank you for speaking with me."

Polly's face tightened. "I figured the alternative would be less pleasant."

"I can attest to that," Anthony chimed in.

Polly maneuvered toward another trio of guests, leaving me alone with Anthony.

"You certainly seem to have charmed her," Anthony commented.

"Really? I'd hate to see her when she's pissed off."

He chuckled. "Trust me. I'm shocked she didn't grab you by the ear and toss you out personally."

I glanced down at my necklace and said a silent prayer of thanks.

"I hope you're not causing trouble in Savannah, Anthony," I said.

"Me? No. I've mended my ways."

I eyed him closely.

He held up his hands in acquiescence. "I'm serious. As a show of good faith, I might be able to offer a bit of helpful information."

I looked at him askance. "And why would you do that?"

"Bygones, Katherine. Surely you don't think I'd hold a grudge."

"Why not? I would."

He flicked a fang with his fingers. "These replacements are far superior to my original set. I should thank you, really."

I wasn't sure whether I trusted him, but I decided to play along. "Let's hear it then."

"Jekyll Island."

"What about it?"

"There's someone on the island who attended the tea party."

"Percival. Been there. Got the T-shirt. Anything else?"

Anthony's mouth turned down at the corners. He seemed genuinely disappointed. "That's all I have. I'll think on it."

"Why help me at all?"

"Truth be told, I dislike the idea that someone has killed one of us with such brutality and gotten away with it. I want them caught as much as you do."

"So if she'd been killed less brutally—say poisoned—you wouldn't bother to help?"

"She was one of the few true queens left in Savannah. If someone as high-profile as Dottie Neff can be slaughtered at her own party, we're all at risk."

"Who's at risk?" Palmer appeared beside me and attempted to slide an arm along my waist.

"None of your business." I pushed his hand away, keeping my focus on Anthony. "It was good to see you again. I'm glad you're doing well."

A hint of a smile formed on his lips. "I don't believe that, but I'll pretend if you will."

Palmer lit up. "This has the markings of an interesting reunion. What did I miss?"

Wordlessly I took a flute from a nearby tray and walked away. Palmer trailed behind me.

"Seriously, what did I miss?"

I swallowed a mouthful of champagne. "Once upon a time

I bashed Anthony in the face with an oxygen tank and knocked out six of his teeth."

"I'm sure he deserved it."

"He did." He'd posed as a doctor in order to siphon blood from unconscious hospital patients. He hadn't been my assignment—we'd simply crossed paths during the course of another investigation. I'd tried to turn him in, but he had friends in high places who let him off with a warning.

Palmer touched his fangs. "I hope you're never that angry with me."

"Not stalking me would be a good start." I sipped my champagne.

He towered over me. "You went to Jekyll Island without me."

I sighed. "How much did you hear?"

"Percival Mulgrew. You got a T-shirt."

"Your hearing is better than I expected."

He grinned. "A lot of me is better than you expect. Why don't you come to my room and I'll show you?"

I ignored him and drained the remainder of champagne.

Palmer plucked the flute from my hand and placed it on a passing tray. "Care to dance?"

"I don't think that's a good idea."

"I didn't say it was. I merely asked if you'd like to." He nodded to the floor. "Even if you don't, those shoes are dying to take a spin. Do it for them. My guess is they've been locked up in your closet for years."

And here I thought the necklace was supposed to make *me* more agreeable. It seemed to be making Palmer more agreeable instead.

"Fine. One dance, but only so I can get closer to Polly. She dodged me earlier and I have more questions to ask."

He slipped an arm around my waist and I ignored the tingling sensation in my abdomen. It wasn't Palmer himself that prompted such feelings. It was simply the touch of a strange man. Any man, really. It had nothing at all to do with the vampire's broad shoulders and rugged jawline. Nor his appealing scent. It had to be the Green Witch in me that responded to the dark and earthy combination of sandalwood and cinnamon.

He leaned down and whispered in my ear, "You feel stiff."

"I thought that was my line." The words shot out of my mouth before I could stop them and my cheeks started to burn. Where did that response come from? Great Goddess, I didn't want him to think I was flirting with him.

I did not flirt.

His mouth quirked. "We could dance a little closer if you'd like to know."

I widened my arms so that I was barely touching him. "Spaghetti arms."

He inclined his head. "I beg your pardon?"

I placed my palm flat on his shoulder as we continued to dance. "Tell me you've never seen Dirty Dancing."

"I haven't, but the title has a certain appeal." He edged closer and I adjusted his stance again.

"This is my space," I said, motioning between us. "This is your space."

"Have you always been this bossy?"

"Have you always been this presumptuous?"

"You should consider yoga. It might help loosen your tight hips."

I peered up at him. "You're a physical therapist now, too?"

"I'm a man of many talents, I think you'll find, some of which might help your hip issue."

My face hardened. "I don't have a hip issue."

He squeezed my waist. "I beg to differ."

"Over to Polly, please," I said through gritted teeth. The hostess was dancing with a man in a blue velvet tuxedo and she didn't look happy about it. If I maneuvered over there now, she might be more willing to talk to me.

Palmer glided us in Polly's direction. "Is it true what they say about Dark Hollow?"

"That depends. What do they say?"

"That it has a mind of its own. Sprouted from the ground one day like lava from a volcano and never left."

"It's enchanted, yes. As for the rest, no one really knows."

"I'd love to see it sometime."

"I don't think so. The house senses unwelcome visitors."

He smirked. "And here I thought we were at the beginning of a beautiful friendship."

"Why have you taken such an interest in me and my family?"

"I told you. Knowledge is power."

"Power is power."

He bent his head closer to mine. "I'd love to see exactly how powerful you are."

I drew back. "Why?"

"Because I find powerful women interesting."

"Dottie Neff was powerful."

He pulled a face. "Not compared to you. She was a molehill."

"And what? I'm a mountain?"

"You're the Alps, darling."

I narrowed my eyes at him. "Who hired you?"

"I told you that's confidential."

"Maybe it's relevant to the case."

"I assure you it isn't. You have my word."

"Can you steer me to Polly, please? You keep veering away."

He turned me away from Polly toward another corner of the room. "Oh, that's because I've already spoken to her. She has an alibi."

"The tennis tournament, I know. It doesn't mean she didn't hire someone to do the deed."

"That was not an assassin's work."

"The head was left on a statue. None of the suspects I've met so far seem cruel enough to plant her head on a statue. It's a strange additional step."

"Exactly. A hired gun would never take the time. This isn't a mafia hit we're dealing with. It's the work of a sociopath."

"So Polly hired a sociopath."

He locked eyes with me. "Or the killer was sending a message. Like when they'd put heads on spikes outside city gates."

"Then what's the message? Show off your magic and this is what will happen to you? The only ones who would care enough about her excessive use of magic would be the council and the FBM."

"Neither of which includes Polly."

I had to admit, I enjoyed talking through the case with someone else. If only that someone else weren't a mysterious vampire with an ego the size of Alaska.

"Do you really think Polly murdered her social rival because they clashed over party schedules?"

"If you're so sure she didn't, then why are you here?"

He grinned. "To see you in a dress. Why else?" Without warning he dipped me and I felt something tweak in my back. I swallowed a cry of pain as he returned me to an upright position. I was woefully out of shape.

"I don't have time to waste, Just Palmer."

"You didn't waste time. You've spoken to Polly and ruled out another suspect. It's all part of the investigative process."

He was right, which only served to annoy me.

I tried to draw magical energy from the necklace. "Tell me who you are and why you're really interested in this case."

Palmer gazed at me with something bordering on affection. "Be the first to solve it and I'll tell you."

Groaning in exasperation, I pushed against his chest. "Thank you for the dance. I think we're done here."

I hiked up my dress so as not to trip and headed for the exit. This time, thankfully, he didn't follow.

CHAPTER ELEVEN

The next morning I chose to interview Rufus Mulgrew. The 'happy' mage lived in a modest, single-story house outside the city center. The building was comprised of the same red brick and white shutters as every other house on the block. As I approached the door, I checked over my shoulder to see whether Palmer had followed me. I cursed under my breath for thinking of him now. The vampire hadn't managed to pierce my skin, but he was certainly getting under it.

Rufus answered the door before I even had a chance to lower my hand from knocking. Although he shared Daisy's coloring, his build was more muscular. Thanks to a pair of black gym shorts and a white tank top, his larger muscle groups were on display.

"Rufus Mulgrew?"

"That's right. You must be the detective. My sister mentioned you might be paying me a visit soon."

Despite the muscles, I wouldn't have considered him attractive until he smiled. He had the kind of smile that seemed to rearrange his facial features.

"I'm Agent Fairfield," I said, shaking his hand.

"Come in. I'm sorry for the mess. I fully intended to clean today, but I ended up working out instead as a way of dealing with my grief." He gestured to his gym shorts and tank top. "Haven't managed a shower yet either. I hope it isn't a problem. I can open the windows. It's nice outside."

"It is."

He darted to the nearest window and pushed it up. "Can I get you something to drink? I don't have a huge selection. Water. Gatorade. Protein shakes." He laughed. "Can you tell I don't entertain very often?"

"Not like Dottie then."

He removed his sneakers and kicked them aside. "No, but then who is? Dottie cared more about entertaining than anybody I've ever met."

"I don't need a drink, but thank you."

Rufus dropped onto the sofa cushion and peeled off his sweaty socks, tossing them on top of the sneakers. "Have a seat."

He wasn't wrong about the mess. The mantel above the fireplace was crammed with knickknacks, although the lone plant seemed to be thriving. There was an empty glass and a plate with crumbs on the coffee table. A stack of men's fitness magazines rested beside the plate. I wouldn't have guessed Daisy's brother would be a gym rat. Then again, my sisters and I had different interests. I liked to read on occasion, but I wasn't obsessed with books like Elizabeth. And Grace...Well, Grace wasn't like either one of us.

"How do we do this?" Rufus asked. "You ask questions and I answer them?"

"Pretty much. It should be relatively painless—far less pain than your workout, I bet."

He cracked another smile and I was once again amazed by the change. No wonder he had a reputation for being happy.

I'd smile incessantly, too, if I knew the effect it had on my countenance.

"No pain, no gain, right? Some guys are born with muscles. Some of us have to work for them. I don't mind, though. Sweat equity builds character. That's what my dad used to say."

I pulled out my pen and notebook. "Tell me about the tea party. I understand you were invited, but not Daisy."

His smile faded. "That's why I was on the fence whether to go. I wanted to boycott on her behalf, but Daisy told me not to be silly. She thinks it's important for me to stay active."

I motioned to his attire. "Seems like you don't have an issue with that."

"She means socially active. If I were left to my own devices, I'd probably exercise, work, and come home. Dottie's social events forced me out of my comfort zone."

"Then you must've liked the fact that the tea party was in costume. You could hide but still be present."

He tugged his ear. "I'll admit, it was a plus. I only went because Daisy insisted, though. I hadn't planned ahead, which is why I dressed as Henry VII. I knew the theme was Wonderland, but whatever. I knew Dottie wouldn't care once she knew it was me."

I laughed. "Why Henry VII?"

"Because I already had the costume from a theater production."

"Shakespeare?"

Rufus shook his head. "The Bard didn't write a play about Henry VII. Too boring. This play was written by a buddy of mine."

"If the subject was too dull for Shakespeare, then why did your friend bother?" I paused, remembering one of Elizabeth's dinnertime lectures during her Tudor phase. "Isn't Henry VII the guy who ended the War of the Roses?" The

Houses of Lancaster and York had been fighting for a century until Henry Tudor came along. He defeated Richard III on the battlefield and seized the throne.

"Exactly. He didn't start a civil war. He ended one." Rufus tipped back his head and pretended to snore. "Nobody wants that."

"So your friend managed to create a version that was more interesting than the truth?"

"I didn't say I agreed with Shakespeare's assessment. I find the whole affair fascinating. Family dramas usually are."

I smiled, thinking of my own family. "We're in agreement on that."

"Is that why you participate in plays? Another way to force yourself out of your comfort zone?" People tend to think of actors as extroverts, but I knew plenty of actors who were introverts.

Rufus nodded. "Gets me out of my own head when I inhabit a character. I find it a relief to be someone else for a little while."

"You might want to try a more upbeat play next time. Henry VII hardly seems like a head you'd want to dwell in."

He slouched against the back of the sofa. "You should've seen Dottie's face when I sat down next to her and tried to pick up one of those tiny teacups while wearing a suit of armor." He barked a laugh. "She couldn't stop laughing."

"Sounds like you were good at entertaining each other."

"I wasn't doing it on purpose, though. She just found me funny." His eyes glazed over. "I'm going to miss that. She was my best audience. Probably one of the reasons I made the effort to attend those stupid parties."

"Talk to me about the family dynamics. How did Dottie manage to live so lavishly at Magnolia Hall? I initially thought Neff might be a married name, but it isn't."

Rufus shook his head. "She never married. She used 'Ms.'

because she thought it made her sound more mysterious." He ran his hands down his face. "Gods, what a drama queen. She was one-of-a-kind."

"If she didn't marry into money, then how? According to my notes, Dottie didn't work either."

"Because she didn't have to. Her branch of the family fared a bit better than the rest of ours. Generational wealth is alive and well in our circles."

"Any resentment among other members of the family?"

"I haven't given it much thought. Money's never been high on my list of priorities. I take what I'm given, of course, but I've never gone out of my way for it."

He and Daisy were alike in that regard. "Is that why your sister's content to live in a shoebox?"

He snorted with laughter. "It's a small place, isn't it? She keeps it real nice, though. Daisy has great taste."

"It's utterly charming," I agreed. "Your place is nice, too. That's a good-looking Aframomum melegueta you've got there."

"I thought it was called an alligator pepper plant. That's why Daisy bought it for me as a housewarming present. She liked the name."

"Congratulations. When did you move in?"

"I guess it was just over a year ago. The fact that I've kept it alive this long is amazing." He turned to admire the potted plant atop the mantel. "It helps that she stops by to water it for me. She said it's the plant version of a wishing star. Supposed to bring good luck."

"That's one of its associations. It's also connected to divination, love, money."

He pinned me with a broad smile. In that brief moment, I understood his good-natured reputation. "You know a lot about plants."

"I'm a Green Witch."

He whistled. "Lucky you. Our family's magic is too watered down to identify a specialty. Even Dottie, although she was the most powerful in our family."

I nodded toward the pink bonsai tree at the opposite end of the mantel. It stood about ten inches tall with a sturdy base made out of the same gemstone as the tiny leaves. "Is that rose quartz?"

Rufus cast a quick glance at the mantel. "Good eye."

"My sister went through a pink quartz phase. At one point her room sparkled so much, you needed sunglasses to enter."

"That piece represents our family tree. It was Dottie's housewarming gift. She knew better than to think I could take care of a plant. Daisy's more optimistic." He released a soft breath. "I'll think of Dottie whenever I look at it."

"It's beautiful. Do you know the origin?"

"Other than it's a family heirloom, no. I should probably keep it somewhere safe, but I like having it in the room where I spend most of my time."

"It definitely looks breakable. What did she give Daisy as a housewarming present?"

He dropped his gaze to the floor. "She wasn't really generous when it came to the others. Like I said, she found me amusing. I guess I reaped the rewards of that over the years."

"Her generosity wasn't limited to heirlooms?"

He raked a hand through his hair, still slick with sweat. "The more I talk, the guiltier I feel. Yeah, she paid for things here and there, mostly my extracurriculars."

"Like your gym membership?"

"All my athletics. I participated in everything under the sun—rugby, lacrosse, fencing, swimming, track." He snorted. "If there was a team to join, I was on it and Dottie agreed to pay for it."

"Did you ask or did she just offer?"

"A mix. Whether she said yes depended on her mood, really. I had to catch her in the right one, or the answer wasn't just no, it was a main course of no with a side of vengeance."

"Sounds delightful."

He chuckled. "She was a piece of work, no arguments there." His expression darkened. "Still hard to believe she's gone. You think someone as formidable as Dottie is destined to live forever."

Again, my thoughts turned to my own family. As powerful as the Fairfield witches were, they were still mortal. They could—and did—die.

Rufus leaned forward and linked his fingers together. "I'd like to say this will bring the family closer together, but who knows? People react differently to death and grief."

"Do you think her will holds any surprises?"

"Not for me. I can't speak for the others, though. I suspect Clement will be disappointed. Dottie wouldn't bother trying to placate him. She knew he'd be miserable about the outcome no matter what it was, so there was no point in trying."

"Clement is another cousin?"

He nodded. "You could show him the most beautiful sunset and he'd ask why it had to be pink instead of orange. He inherited that attitude from his mom. She was a real Debbie Downer."

"Would you mind telling me where I can find Clement? He's on my list."

"Figured he would be. He may be a grouch, but he's no killer."

"I'll keep that in mind," I said, as I scribbled down the information he gave me. "Do you have any theories about Dottie's death?"

"Are you asking me to name a suspect?" Shaking his head,

he waved his hands. "No way. I'm not pointing the finger at anybody in my family."

"So you think it's likely a Mulgrew."

"No, I didn't say that." He seemed flustered. "Dottie was the kind of woman who had enemies. When you're that rich and powerful and dramatic, you tend to draw attention to yourself, but I can't think of anybody who'd actually kill her because of those things. It was more like don't invite her to your barbecue or your baby shower."

I scribbled a few notes.

He smiled. "Are you writing down everything I say? You know you could just record it on your phone, right?"

"I could, but I like to write down observational details as well. What I see. First impressions, that sort of thing."

"I hope you don't apply the same process to dating. If a woman whipped out a notebook, I'd be out of there."

Laughing, I tucked away my notebook and rose to my feet. I was mildly embarrassed when my knees cracked.

Rufus smiled. "That means you've got carbon dioxide built up in the joint. That sound is a gas bubble bursting."

Terrific, so I basically passed gas in front of him. "Did you learn that from your trainer?"

"No, my cousin Luke. He's a doctor."

"Another cousin."

"Yep. We're like rats in this city. We keep multiplying." He jumped to his feet, impressively energetic considering the recent workout. I should be that fit. "Are you sure I can't get you a drink or anything before you go?"

"No, thank you. If you think of anything that might help the case, will you give me a call?" I passed my card to him.

He glanced at the card as he escorted me to the door. "Katherine's a pretty name. I feel like it's one of those names that never goes out of style. Not like Rufus, which was never in style in case you were wondering."

I laughed again. "I won't tell you about the Doberman Pinscher named Rufus I knew. He was not a particularly nice dog."

He closed his eyes in mortification. "Please don't."

"It was nice to meet you, Rufus. Best of luck to you."

"Best of luck with the case. I really hope you find out who did this to Dottie. Give our family closure."

"I'll do my best."

As I walked along the pathway, I pondered the information I learned. Clement was next on my list of suspects. He sounded like the opposite of Rufus, although I was determined to keep an open mind.

Labels were a funny thing. It seemed to me that Daisy wasn't that dopey and Rufus wasn't that happy, nor was Percival as shy and withdrawn as everyone thought.

It was time to find out if Clement was as grumpy as his cousins believed.

CHAPTER TWELVE

I double-checked the address on Jones Street. Every home here was spectacular. Even the wide, brick-paved street was beautiful. I would've gladly lived in any of the homes I passed. Stopping in front of Clement's house, I held the same opinion. This house was much nicer than the ones owned by Daisy and Rufus.

The sound of someone grunting in exertion drew my attention to the narrow side yard where a man was splitting wood with an axe. This was the type of guy Rufus meant when he said some guys were born with muscles. His broad shoulders and powerful biceps were accentuated by a tight black T-shirt. The band of his jeans rested on his hips. As he raised the axe, his tank top rode up and I caught a glimpse of a six-pack. Good thing Grace wasn't here. She'd already be perched on the log for a better view.

I entered through the open gate. "Excuse me. Are you Clement Mulgrew?"

He lowered the axe with a scowl already in place. "Who wants to know?"

"My name is Agent Katherine Fairfield."

His scowl deepened. "Yankee."

I tried to diffuse the tension. "Are you calling me a candle?"

He leaned his palm on the handle of the axe. "I don't like funny women. They're like a crime against nature."

To be fair, the joke wasn't funny, but it was the first response that came to mind. "I'm with the Federal Bureau of Magic."

He spat on the ground. "I don't like cops."

I ignored him. "I'd like to talk to you..."

"About the death of my cousin. Blah blah. I know the spiel."

An image of Palmer flashed in my mind. "Someone's already spoken to you?"

"No, but it wouldn't be the first police interview I've been subject to."

According to the file, his record was clean so whatever he'd been suspected of, he hadn't been arrested for it.

I gestured to his hand. "Would you mind putting down the axe while we talk?"

His gaze lingered on the axe for a prolonged moment. Despite his air of hostility, he let the axe fall to the ground. "Pull up a tree stump. Let's talk."

I concentrated on the smallest stump in the yard and formed a connection. I dragged the stump toward me and sat.

Clement gaped at me. "Nice trick."

"One of the perks of being a Green Witch." I angled my head toward the house. "Your place is beautiful."

"Wish it was mine. A friend owns it as an investment property and lets me live here at a reduced rate, as long as I help out with yard work and general maintenance."

That explained it. "Must've been difficult to visit Dottie and see how extravagantly your cousin lived while you're having to rent a place that's not nearly as nice."

Clement's upper lip curled. "Are you kidding me? This house is much better than that pile of putrid bricks she lived in. The inside of her house gives me a headache, not unlike the woman herself." He waved a hand at the nearest wall. "Check out that ivy and those dormers. Magnolia Hall don't hold a Yankee candle to this house." A slow grin emerged. "You see what I did there? Now that's funny."

"Very clever, Mr. Mulgrew, and I agree with you—about the house." I held out my hand. "I think we may have gotten off on the wrong foot. Why don't we try this again? I'm Agent Fairfield with the FBM."

He shook my hand. His grip was every bit as firm as I expected. I winced as he squeezed harder.

Mocking laughter rang out when he noticed my expression. "I would've thought the FBM would want their agents to be strong. I guess Dottie wasn't important enough to get the best agent on her case. Boy, she'd hate to know that." He laughed again, still maintaining a tight grip on my hand.

Clement Mulgrew was more than grumpy. He was downright sadistic, which now made him my number one suspect.

Using my free hand, I pushed him with as much force as I could muster. The move surprised him. He let go of my hand and stumbled back to the wall of the house. I commandeered the ivy and used the sturdy vines to secure him there.

"Another perk of being a Green Witch," I said.

He appeared unfazed. His smile was nothing like his cousin's. Rufus's smile was warm and welcoming, whereas Clement's was cold and cruel, more like an angry dog showing its teeth. He seemed awfully hostile for an innocent man. Now that I'd asserted my dominance, maybe I could persuade him to answer my questions, preferably without the attitude.

"Now how'd you know I liked to be tied up? You're just full of cute tricks, aren't you?"

"I'm full of questions, too. Why don't we get started?"

The sooner I got answers, the sooner I could put distance between us.

"Looks like you've made a new friend," a voice said.

I twisted to see Palmer standing at the open gate. "Seriously? Are you stalking me again?"

The vampire chuckled. "Wishful thinking, Ms. Fairfield."

"*Agent* Fairfield."

"Is this your boyfriend?" Clement asked. "I should've known they wouldn't send a woman to do a job like this by herself. Your little gardening act will only get you so far."

I twirled my finger and watched with satisfaction as a thick vine slid into his mouth and wrapped around his head like a gag.

I turned back to Palmer. "Do you mind? I'm in the middle of an interview."

"And I can see it's going very well for you." He strode forward. "This is Clement Mulgrew, I take it."

Clement responded, not that we could understand him.

"Yes."

Palmer tilted his head to examine the suspect. "One of the servers said she overheard Clement shouting at Dottie at the tea party and was asked to leave. Did he tell you about that?"

Clement had been thrown out of the party for yelling at Dottie? Why had no one mentioned that? Blood was thicker than legal trouble, it seemed.

"We were just getting to that." I twirled my finger again to remove the vine from the mage's mouth. "Care to offer your version of events, Mr. Mulgrew?"

He glared at me. "So I got kicked out. Big deal. Wouldn't be the first time. Dottie said I was bringing down the vibe with my bad attitude."

"And were you?" Palmer asked.

I gave the vampire an incredulous look. "Listen to him. Do you really need to ask?"

Clement pursed his lips, looking every inch the sour apple they accused him of being. "The music was garbage and the bartender sucked."

I looked at Palmer who seemed slightly amused by the admission.

"People don't typically fight with the hostess over the choice of music and the quality of service," I pointed out.

"The music was jazz—Dottie knows how much I hate jazz—and the bar didn't stock any beer. Dottie knows that's all I drink."

Palmer studied him. "And you think your cousin played jazz and withheld beer from the party menu solely to put the screws to you? In that case, why invite you at all?"

"She enjoyed pressing my buttons," Clement said. "She pulled crap like that since I was a kid. Thought it was funny to watch me go ballistic and then react like it's such a big surprise when I get upset."

Based on what I'd learned about Dottie Neff, the information seemed plausible.

"Then why show up if you knew this would happen?" Palmer pressed.

Clement looked away. "Because."

"Very illuminating," Palmer murmured.

I latched on to a theory. "Maybe you got there thinking this time would be different. Maybe Dottie even promised it would be. When it wasn't, you flew into a rage and killed her. I've already seen how handy you are with an axe. Maybe we should test it for Dottie's blood."

"I didn't bring an axe to the party. I dressed as the Knave of Hearts."

I folded my arms. "The Knave of Hearts carries a sword."

"Mine wasn't sharp enough to cut through a hunk of

cheese, let alone a head. It's our family's ceremonial sword. I keep it on the wall above the fireplace like a decoration."

"I'd like to see it before I go."

"And I'm still interested in why you would show up to an event that you knew would upset you," Palmer added.

Clement licked his lips. "I showed up because the other members of my family were going to be there, except Daisy. I happen to like my cousins."

"Except Dottie," I said. "I find it hard to believe you'd like a woman who treated you so horribly, whether she was related to you or not." Mainly because he didn't seem to like women at all.

"No, I didn't care for her, but she had the money and the magic in the family, so she was the glue that held us together whether we liked it or not." He tried to tug his arms forward. "Would you mind letting me go? I promise I won't pull any stunts. Anyway, even if I do, your boyfriend's here to protect you now."

I tried not to let my irritation show. It would give Palmer too much pleasure.

I twirled my finger in the air and the vines slithered back to the wall. Clement's boots hit the ground with a thud, but he remained standing.

"Look, I can't pretend to be sad she's gone, but I didn't kill her. Like I said, she was the glue and I like the rest of my family. Truth is, without Dottie's gatherings, I don't know how often we'll see each other now. It's a loss for me any which way you look at it."

"You could make your own arrangements," I said. "The fate of the family doesn't need to rely on one person."

"No, I guess not. We just got in the habit of letting Dottie dictate the terms of our get-togethers. It'll be nice to include Daisy again. She's a sweet kid. Dottie was so jealous of her." He used the toe of his boot to shift a log aside.

"You think Dottie was jealous of her?"

"Oh, yeah. Of Daisy and Bex. Not so much Lauren. No offense to her. She's nice enough."

"Why Bex?" I asked.

"She's prettier than Daisy. Smarter, too. A little lazy, though. If you ask me, it was mainly Daisy that Dottie felt threatened by."

"Daisy seems so easygoing and carefree. Why would Dottie feel threatened by her?"

"That's it right there. Because everybody liked Daisy for just being Daisy. She didn't have to prove nothing to nobody."

"Whereas Dottie felt that she had to throw a party or spend money or show off her magic to be worthy of her relationships," Palmer said.

"Exactly." Clement pointed at the vampire. "See? He gets it."

"I get it, too," I said, bristling.

"Daisy was a breath of fresh air, but Dottie was like a cold wind that gives you the chills."

"We get the picture," I said. "Do you think this idea of Dottie being fed up with Daisy's poor judgment is inaccurate?"

"No, but I think Dottie used that as an excuse to bully her. She could hardly exclude Daisy on the basis of everybody liking her. Then she'd have to admit how it made her feel."

It made sense.

"Did Dottie ever give you gifts or pay any bills for you?" I asked.

Clement allowed himself a tiny smile. "Do I look like Rufus to you? No, ma'am. She did not, except on birthdays. Then she'd send over a new toolkit or a gift card to one of the local restaurants. Nothing fancy."

"What about your magic?" I asked.

Clement narrowed his eyes. "What about it?"

"If Daisy's is the weakest and Dottie's was the strongest, where do you fit in?"

Clement cracked his knuckles. "Couldn't say. I don't go showing off like some folks." He gave me a pointed look.

"If you don't mind satisfying my curiosity, what is it you can do?" Palmer interrupted.

Clement shifted his weight from foot to foot. "I'm a one-trick pony. Nothing like this Green Witch here. Mages aren't that powerful in general."

"Magi," Palmer corrected him.

Clement looked at him askance. "Is that the plural?"

"If it isn't, it should be," Palmer said in a clipped tone.

Clement blew out a breath. "I'm telekinetic. Like this." He focused his attention on the axe. The handle lifted off the ground first. "Sometimes I do maintenance this way—use telekinesis to control the tools while I drink a beer or something."

"Can you lift a sword?" Palmer and I asked in unison.

We turned to look at each other.

"This is my interview," I said firmly. I shifted my attention back to Clement. If he was able to control a sword from a short distance, he could've easily hidden across the courtyard and attacked Dottie without being seen.

Clement scrunched his face. "Is it a sword that killed her? I heard they hadn't identified the murder weapon."

"They narrowed it down to a sharp blade," I said.

"Well, a butter knife is technically a blade," Clement replied.

"I can assure you it wasn't a butter knife," Palmer said. "Now answer the question."

"Yeah, of course I can operate a sword with my mind. It's no heavier than the axe."

"I'd like to see that sword now," I told him. "I'll wait here."

To my surprise, he didn't argue. He retreated into the house.

"You're very trusting," Palmer said. "What if he runs off?"

"Then he won't get far," I said, as I jotted down the salient details of our conversation in my notebook.

The ends of his mouth twitched. "Because your New Balance sneakers help you run like the wind?"

I ignored him as Clement returned with the sword in hand. I had him place it on the grass between us. I tested the sword for any physical evidence using an herbal concoction I kept in my bag. Science was helpful, but magic was better in a pinch.

"What's that stuff called?" Clement asked as he watched me wipe down the blade.

"It's a homemade blend I call Reveal." I returned to an upright position.

Clement's biceps bulged as he folded his arms and looked at me. "Does this mean I'm under arrest?"

"No."

Palmer pivoted to face me. "No?"

I shook my head. "There's nothing on the sword."

"Because he cleaned it," Palmer said.

"Except it isn't clean. There are traces of dirt and dust."

Clement seemed relieved.

I made a few notes and tucked away the notebook as well as the small container of Reveal. "Your record was clean when I looked. Why were you interviewed by the police before?"

Hesitation flickered in Clement's eyes. "Somebody stole an obelisk and they had reason to believe I was involved."

"An obelisk?" I echoed.

He nodded. "It was on the grave of one of those slave traders. Used his money from buying and selling slaves to purchase himself a big, ugly monument as a testament to his wealth. Someone who found this distasteful *may* have taken the obelisk and disposed of it in the river."

"But that someone wasn't you," I said.

"No, ma'am. My muscles are strong, but I'm not Superman."

"What about your mind?" I asked. "The brain is a muscle, too."

Clement's smirk dissipated as quickly as it appeared. "Is it? I had no idea."

I retrieved a card from my pocket and offered it to him. "If you think of anything helpful, will you get in touch?"

Clement tucked the card in his back pocket without looking at it. "Sure thing. Can I get back to work now? These logs aren't going to chop themselves." He grinned. "Or are they?"

CHAPTER THIRTEEN

I sat at the dining table in The Springhouse, reviewing my notes. Clement was still high on my list of suspects, but was someone who was so outraged by a slave trader's monument that he used telekinesis to rip it out of the ground the kind of man who would kill his cousin over—what? Bad taste in music? Annoying pranks? Humiliation by a woman seemed to be the strongest motive, but it didn't change the fact that the sword was clean.

"You're deep in thought," Madam Lemonte said, seating herself across from me. "Anything I can do? A peach tart, perhaps?"

"You've fed me enough to survive the winter," I joked. "I think you've done all you can."

I tapped the pen on the edge of the table. There was still the mystery of Palmer to solve as well. I had an imbalance of questions and answers and I didn't like it. I tossed the pen and notebook into my bag and stood.

"Going out?"

"Yes. The reading of the will should be over and I'm meeting the lawyer."

"Sounds promising. Good luck."

I approached George's office promptly at seven. The lawyer stood outside the building smoking a cigarette.

"Before you ask, I have no plans to quit. I've smoked so many years, whatever damage it can do has been done." He dropped the cigarette on the sidewalk and stamped it out. "It's a nice evening and I've been indoors all day. Why don't we walk?"

"Sounds good to me." I was accustomed to a daily dose of the great outdoors thanks to the sanctuary. The animals liked when we paid them attention. We rotated visitation duties to allow time for our other tasks. Just because I was a powerful Green Witch didn't mean I could go without honing my skills. I kept up a regular practice over the years, including a small witch's garden on the balcony by the kitchen where I grew most of the herbs.

"The cousins were all present and accounted for, as I'm sure you expected."

"Daisy?"

He nodded. "Even Percival, although he didn't go out to dinner with the others afterward, though. He said he was headed straight back to the island after so much peopling."

A cool breeze rushed past us and I buttoned my cardigan. "Anything noteworthy?"

"The guest cottage is to remain with the house, although Dottie does request that Mandy be allowed to continue to live in the cottage for as long as she likes."

"It isn't legally enforceable, though."

"No, it's a wish. Nothing more."

"Who gets Magnolia Hall?"

"All seven cousins."

I stopped walking and turned to face him. "She left the estate to all of them? Why?"

George heaved a sigh. "Dottie thought it would be

amusing to let them fight over it. With seven people, there are bound to be disagreements as to whether to sell or not. If they do sell, how much to accept. The possibility for conflict is endless." He slid his hands into his trouser pockets as we continued to walk. "I enjoyed Dottie's company very much, but she could be cruel on occasion."

"I'm surprised she included Daisy. I thought she cut her out of the will."

"She did, except for that part."

"Did you try to talk her out of doing it?"

"It's my job to carry out my client's wishes." He paused in front of a bar. "I'm meeting my wife inside for a drink if you'd care to join us." He smiled wryly. "It was her idea to come here after the reading. She knows me well."

"I'll pass, thanks. Did you notice anything odd during the reading? Any strange reactions?"

He shook his head. "No, and I kept a close watch, too. Daisy was quiet, as expected. Rufus was the de facto leader of the group, also as expected. Percival was pleasantly surprised to be singled out for a family heirloom. I felt happy for the guy." He splayed his hands. "Truth be told, I can't see any of them hurting Dottie. She was, if she'll forgive me for saying so, the worst of them when it came to inflicting pain and suffering."

"If you think of anything, will you let me know?"

"Absolutely." He turned and entered the bar.

I continued to walk, enjoying the fresh air and the charm of old Savannah. Even in the darkness, there was a certain vibrancy to the city. I still had to interview the remaining cousins. It might be easier now that they knew the contents of the will. Maybe they'd have more to say.

I found myself at the river and paused to admire the moonshine on the water. Closing my eyes, I let the magical energy wash over me. As much as I loved Dark Hollow, it felt good to be somewhere else. I'd forgotten how nice a change in environment could be.

"Romantic evening, isn't it?"

I craned my neck to look at him. "How tall are you?"

"Six-four," Palmer replied.

"That's what I thought. You must hit your head on some of these low ceilings."

He smiled. "I'm not staying in a hobbit house." He shifted his gaze back to the moonlight and whistled. "All seven cousins are getting the house, huh? It's certainly big enough for them."

"I guess you were eavesdropping on my conversation with George."

"Can I help it if I happen to be within range of an interesting discussion? If you wanted to keep your conversation secret, you should've had it indoors."

I stifled a laugh. "Then I picture you outside with a glass pressed to the wall."

He rocked back and forth on the balls of his feet. "I would never stoop to such a level." He paused. "I'd simply break in quietly and listen at the door."

"I've been going back through my conversations with everyone. You spoke to Daisy. What did you think of her?"

Now it was his turn to suppress a smile. "She's very sweet, isn't she?"

"And did you rule her out based on sweetness?"

"There's something refreshing about her. Yes, I ruled her out, but not solely because of her lovely disposition."

"I ruled her out, too." There was no point in denying it if we were on the same page.

"Would you like to interview the remaining three cousins together?" he asked.

"I don't think so."

"Because you work alone?"

"Because I work with seasoned professionals, of which you are not."

"I'm quite professional."

"A professional pain in the ass, maybe."

He clutched his chest. "I'm truly offended."

I smirked. "Yes, I can see that."

"You're warming to me, aren't you? I'm thawing that thick layer of ice. I'm like the Titanic slicing right through that iceberg." He made a slicing motion with his hand.

I gave him a sidelong look. "I think you'll find the iceberg sank the Titanic."

His eyebrows drew together. "Right. But still. The iceberg has been one huge chunk of ice and suddenly it's split into pieces."

"You might want to come up with another metaphor for our relationship."

His face brightened. "Ah, so it's a relationship already. My, you do move quickly, don't you? I would've waited at least a month to define it as a relationship, though I guess it depends." He pivoted toward me. "Are we sleeping together yet? Or are we waiting until the honeymoon? I'm traditional but not *that* traditional."

I rolled my eyes and retreated from the river.

Palmer quickly followed. "You can't blame me, Agent Fairfield. A romantic moonlight stroll along the river with a beautiful, talented woman such as yourself. I'd be a fool if I didn't try."

"I didn't invite you to join me. As usual, you just turned up like a bad penny."

"There's a coin shortage. I think you'll discover all pennies are good now."

I pressed my lips together. "I'm going back to my room now. Good night, Palmer."

"Sleep well, Agent Fairfield. Pleasant dreams. Perhaps think of me as you're falling asleep. That'll help."

Groaning, I picked up the pace.

There were several tour groups hogging the sidewalks, so I took a detour through a cemetery. Colonial Park served as the primary cemetery in the city between 1750 and 1853. It was no longer an active cemetery, which meant I could cut through without interruption.

Well, without interruption from the living.

Out of the corner of my eye, I spotted an ethereal figure.

"There are plenty of tourists to spook," I said, jabbing a thumb over my shoulder. "If you're lucky, maybe one of them can see you."

"Beg your pardon, miss. You're not with the ghost tour then?"

I stopped walking and pivoted toward the friendly ghost. "No, I'm taking a shortcut."

The ghost floated back behind a gravestone. "Oopsie. I'll just wait back here until it's time. Sorry to disturb you. Carry on."

I pinned him with a hard stare. "Time for what?"

"The tour operator brings people by. Likes us to pop out now and again. Sometimes there's a human in the group that doesn't know they have the Sight." The ghost chuckled softly. "Hilarious. Makes it worth climbing out of the coffin."

I guess they had to humor themselves somehow. My ancestors were fortunate to have us at Dark Hollow.

I cut a glance at the sidewalk. There was no sign of the group yet. Or Palmer.

"If you notice a vampire following me, will you let me know?"

"Any vampire or one in particular?"

"One in particular. He goes by Palmer like he's some sort of celebrity everybody knows. The ego on that one..."

The ghost shuddered and slipped behind a gravestone.

I frowned. "Was it something I said?"

"Palmer. You said Palmer," his voice rang out.

I peered around the corner of the headstone. "I can still see you."

The ghost turned his pleading eyes to me. "Mr. Death is in Savannah? Why?"

"Mr. Death? That's what you call Palmer? Is it because he's a vampire?"

The ghost's teeth rattled.

My hands moved to my hips. "How are you making that sound? You're incorporeal. You don't have any bones."

He pointed at the ground. "They're in there. I'm basically a ventriloquist throwing my voice outside the coffin."

Delightful.

The ghost raised a shaky finger. "You might want to look behind you, miss."

"Ha! I'm not falling for that trick."

Something hard made contact with the back of my head. I lurched forward and grabbed two headstones to keep myself from face-planting. I barely had time to recover before my assailant hit me again. I felt the movement of air to my left and staggered to the right. They clipped my shoulder and pain jolted me. I forced myself to run. I couldn't let the third time be the charm.

I sprinted through the cemetery, sticking to the main path that was illuminated by streetlights. My head and shoulder throbbed. I couldn't run for much longer. For one thing, I was forty-four and woefully out of practice. My exercise routine generally involved chasing animals around the sanctuary and lifting piles of laundry. Once upon a time, I was 'the fastest wand in the West' as Martin used to call me. It was a nonsensical label as I neither lived on the West Coast nor used a wand. Still, the nickname stuck and newer agents would occasionally stop me in the hallway to marvel at my moniker.

Part of me longed to turn and confront my attacker but thoughts of Imogen and Deacon prevented me from taking any unnecessary risks. They'd already lost their father.

I'd been foolish to agree to this job. Hex Support was inherently dangerous and I knew it. Why did I agree to take the case?

Pain stabbed my chest as I escaped through the open gates and continued running until I reached the street corner. I spared a glance over my shoulder to see whether I'd been followed, but the shadows remained still. Even in my sneakers, I'd suffer from shin splints in the morning, no doubt about it. I rubbed the back of my head and realized part of my hair was matted and sticky.

Blood.

A pair of headlights approached, momentarily blinding me.

A head poked out the driver's side window. "Need a lift, Agent Fairfield?"

I focused on the pickup truck. "Hey, Bert."

He reached across the cab of the truck and opened my door. "Get in. You look like you've been buried and resurrected."

"Gee, thanks." I climbed into the seat and winced as I reached to shut the door.

He drove in the direction of The Springhouse. "I'm going to go out on a limb and say your investigation is still ongoing."

I tugged a twig from my hair and rolled down the window to dispose of it. "It is."

"Should I take you to a healer?"

"I'll be fine."

"Just a flesh wound, right?" He chuckled. "You agent types are all the same." He pulled alongside the curb in front of the safe house. "You take care of yourself, Agent Fairfield."

"Thanks for the ride." I exited the truck and limped inside.

"Rough night, mon cher?" Madam Lemonte asked as I walked slowly past her, trying my best to appear normal.

"Encountered a bit of trouble at Colonial Park."

"Spirits?"

"Somebody attacked me with a tree limb."

She grunted. "I can bring you a cup of herbal tea—or perhaps a nightcap if you would prefer."

"That would be nice, thank you."

"While the kettle is boiling, I'll check your wounds."

"That won't be necessary. I'm fine."

Madam Lemonte pointed to the table and chairs. "Sit."

I sat.

She inspected my head first, then my shoulder. "Looks worse than it is. Let's get you cleaned up."

I drank my tea while she tended to my wounds. Although I didn't love the circumstances, it was nice to have someone else taking care of me for a change. I was accustomed to being the one in charge of everyone else.

Afterward I climbed the flights of stairs, cursing every step. I was a fast healer, but my body was out of practice. The worst I'd encountered in the past ten years was a concussion after Deacon whacked me in the head with a lacrosse ball.

As I opened the door to my room, I sensed something was amiss. I stopped in the doorway and peered inside. Clothing was strewn on the floor and drawers pulled open. The mattress was tipped on its side. Curtains rustled as a breeze blew through the open window. Apparently the third floor had been no deterrent. Then again, there was enough ivy on the outside walls to make it easy for a skilled climber.

Heaving a sigh, I turned around and headed back to Madam Lemonte. She wasn't going to be happy about this. She prided herself on the safety of her guesthouse.

"Mon Dieu," she cried when I shared the news. "But how is this possible?"

"I don't know."

We returned to the scene of the crime and I scoured the room for evidence.

"Did they take anything?"

"Not that I've noticed. They even left the spare cash I had in the top drawer."

Her wary eyes flicked to me. "Perhaps it's a warning."

"I think the warning was issued in the cemetery. This suggests they were on the hunt for something."

"Like what?" She folded a cotton top and placed it neatly on the dresser.

The only item in my possession connected to the case was my notebook, which I kept tucked in my handbag.

"Do you think your friend at Colonial Park was able to follow you here?"

"It's possible." And if they were after my notebook, was it mere curiosity or had I discovered something significant that I hadn't managed to put together yet? The only people who knew about the notebook were those I'd interviewed—unless one of the suspects mentioned my notes to someone I hadn't interviewed yet. There were still three cousins left to interview and the Mulgrews seemed fairly tight-knit.

I didn't feel comfortable staying here right now. "Where's a quiet place I can decompress?"

Madam Lemonte waved a hand at the wall. "Try the bar in the basement of The Olde Pink House. Very cozy. Normally I would recommend my garden, but I don't think that's what you need tonight."

No, it wasn't. I needed to shake off the violation and I couldn't do that if I stayed.

I decided to spend the remainder of the evening reviewing my notes to see what I might've missed. If the notebook was worth beating me for, then it required closer scrutiny.

With the notebook still in my handbag, I left the not-so-safe house and walked to Reynolds Square. Madam Lemonte was right. The bar in the basement of The Olde Pink House was exactly the right atmosphere. Exposed brick. Beamed ceilings. A roaring fire to cut through the evening chill. Leather armchairs. Heaven.

I spotted an available chair by the fireplace and made a beeline for it. I was pleased when the bartender signaled to me from behind the counter. No way was I getting up to order and abandoning my prime location.

I ordered a cocktail called Pink Lady. A sense of calm washed over me as I sipped the libation and flipped through the pages of the notebook.

"Pink suits you," a familiar voice said.

I lifted my gaze to the vampire and my chest constricted. Did he have to look so attractive? It had to be the favorable lighting. His hair was slightly damp, which made me wonder if he'd recently showered. The thought of Palmer in the shower stirred feelings I refused to acknowledge. I shoved the image aside and tried to focus on one of his flaws. I searched his face for something—anything—a birthmark or a hairy mole, but to no avail.

I closed my notebook. "What are you doing here? Oh, wait. *I'm* here. Mystery solved."

He sat in the empty chair across from me. I hadn't

noticed my previous neighbor leave. "This is relaxing. Taking the night off?"

"I'm considering it. I had a rather unfortunate encounter in the cemetery after I left you at the river." I told him about my brush with danger and my ransacked room. I briefly considered withholding the information but ultimately didn't see the point.

His eyebrows drew together. "You must be getting close."

"Or someone is unnecessarily worried and hit the panic button."

"Is that why you're looking through your notes? Because you think someone panicked unnecessarily?"

I remembered the ghost in the cemetery. "Why do people call you Mr. Death?"

His face remained impassive. "Do they?"

Stonewalled again.

A bartender appeared and delivered a cocktail to the vampire.

"Thank you."

I eyed the drink. "That doesn't look like whiskey."

"Because it isn't. It's called Water of Life. Would you like to try it?" He held the glass toward me. "Go on. I'll even let you taste it before I take a drink."

"Such a gentleman. Thanks, but I'll stick to my own drink. There's no way to know whether you asked the bartender to add a special ingredient." I sipped from my own glass.

"You'll never let me live that down, will you?"

I looked at him. "It was uncalled for. When a strange man puts a little something special in a woman's drink, it never ends well."

"It was to elicit information, nothing more."

"I know." I rested my glass on the arm of the chair. "Who taught you about plants anyway?"

"I have many staff members to advise me."

"What kind of staff members? For what?"

He smiled faintly and drank. "Business. Don't you have experts you consult, or at least you must have once upon a time?"

"Of course." His comment sparked an idea.

"Another cocktail for you and the lady, Palmer?" the bartender called from behind the counter.

The vampire offered a brief nod.

"If you don't live here, why does everybody know your name?" I asked.

"I like to cultivate a network everywhere I go."

"A network of sycophants."

His eyes twinkled with amusement. "He's doing his job well. How does that make him a sycophant?" His mouth curved slightly. "Ah, I see. You're showing off your vocabulary to make up for your bad grammar the other night. Not to worry, Ms. Fairfield. You have nothing to prove to me. I have no doubt you're highly intelligent."

I glowered at the vampire. "Your condescending tone suggests otherwise."

He sipped his drink demurely. "This seems to be a sensitive subject for you. What past intellectual trauma have I managed to unlock?"

As the bartender set two fresh cocktails on the table between us, I tore through my handbag in search of pen and paper. "Okay, smarty pants. Let's see who wins in the most intellectual game of all."

He frowned. "Chess?"

I drew a large '7' with a base. "Hangman." When the twins were younger, I spent countless hours playing hangman with them. Elizabeth and Grace, too.

I counted out the letters of my word and marked them on the paper. Then I took a long drink of my cocktail. The Pink

Lady was delicious. I'd have to remember the name for next time.

He studied the blanks on the paper. "Do I get any hints?"

"This isn't remedial hangman. You're in the big leagues now."

"Oh, I see." He hunched over the paper and scrutinized the nine marks. "I guess a single letter at a time?"

"Yes."

"I'll start with an 's.'" He paused to smile at me. "For sycophant." His fangs glinted in the dim light, reminding me that my companion was no ordinary man.

"Hardy har." I drew a double 's' at the end of the word.

"Interesting. I'll say 'w' next."

I drew a head on the hangman's noose.

"You've given me a rather odd-shaped head," he observed. "Almost oval."

"You're stalling. Guess another letter."

"T."

Begrudgingly I wrote the letter 't' in the correct spot.

The cocktail seemed to have emboldened me. "Tell me the real reason you've been skulking around Savannah."

"I already did. I'm investigating on behalf of a private party."

"Your investigation seems to consist of following me around to see what I learned. That sounds like a scavenger. Daisy was the only witness you spoke to before I did."

"She was the obvious choice. 'R.'"

I drew a neck on the stick figure and drank again. "And here I thought you'd have cracked it by now."

He glanced at me. "You're shockingly competitive. I wasn't expecting Monica from *Friends*."

"And I wasn't expecting Joey."

His smile broadened. "Touché, Agent Fairfield."

I straightened in my chair. "You called me 'Agent.'"

"I blame the alcohol. Not to worry. It won't happen again." He pondered the paper. "O."

I added a body to the noose. "Have you discovered any information that I haven't during your non-scavenging hours?"

"If I had, don't you think I would've shared it with you?"

"No."

He peered at the puzzle. "Are you certain this is a word? I think you've invented one just to toy with me."

I smiled. "It's a word and I believe Shakespeare invented it."

"Aha. A clue." He tapped the paper. "H."

I made a buzzing sound and drew the left arm.

"How many parts of me do you draw before it's considered game over?"

"Right arm. Legs."

"No face? What about hair?" He dragged a hand through his thick head of hair. "If I'm going to die, I'd like to look good doing it."

"No hair or face. Let's go, Palmer. Three guesses left." I swigged the cocktail.

"N."

With added flare, I drew the right arm.

"A."

I wrote the letter 'a' in the second spot.

Palmer studied the paper again. "M."

I had to give him credit, he managed to sound smooth and assured even when giving the wrong answers.

Smiling, I drew the left leg first. Victory was within reach.

"If only you solved murder mysteries as well as you play hangman," he remarked.

"Right back at you."

"L. I should've guessed that one already. It's obviously 'less' at the end."

I drew the letter.

He mulled over the missing letters. "Last chance, yes?"

"Yes."

"I."

"Consider yourself hanged." I filled in the remaining letters and turned the paper toward him.

"Dauntless," he read aloud. "Good one."

"Suck it, vampire."

He cocked his head. "That's not the insult you think it is. More of an invitation, really." His gaze flicked to the curve of my neck. "A very appealing one, I might add."

My throat ran dry.

I tipped back the glass and drained the remaining drops of the cocktail. "I should go. Enjoy your Water of Life."

"And here I thought we were enjoying a nice evening together."

I rose to my feet. "We're not doing anything together. Nothing at all."

I felt his eyes tracking me as I crossed the room and a shiver ran through me. I left money on the counter on my way out. I'd return home tonight and regroup. I wanted to give the killer the impression that I'd given up, help them breathe easier before I made another move. Maybe I'd get lucky and they'd show their hand first.

I said goodbye to Madam Lemonte, packed my things, and returned to Dark Hollow.

CHAPTER FOURTEEN

I slept comfortably in my bed and dreamed of skeletons spelling out words with their bones in Bonaventure Cemetery. It was more comical than eerie, especially when they spelled out 'sycophant.' Part of me wanted to share the dream with Palmer, but I quickly dismissed the notion. The vampire and I weren't friends and he was clearly hiding something from me. For all I knew, he was involved in Dottie's murder and stalking me to make sure I didn't figure out the truth. As unlikely as it seemed, I couldn't rule out the possibility.

I ventured downstairs for breakfast with Isis hot on my heels. The cat was annoyed to have been left behind and was letting her feelings be known.

Elizabeth and Grace were already in the kitchen arguing over a pancake recipe. Elizabeth wanted to follow the recipe whereas Grace wanted to wing it. If that didn't describe their personalities perfectly, I didn't know what else did.

"Good morning," I said.

Elizabeth glanced up from the recipe book. "I didn't realize you were back."

"I came back last night. Someone broke into my room at the safe house so I thought it best to come home for now."

"Not very safe for a safe house," Grace said. "Did you tell Martin?"

"I texted him last night."

Elizabeth scrutinized me. "You're standing crooked."

I straightened. "I tweaked my shoulder. It should be fine soon." My head was already back to normal—relatively speaking.

Grace's eyes held a glimmer of suspicion. "Did that vampire hurt you?"

"No. Don't worry about me. It's nothing." I observed the mixing bowl. "Would you like me to take over now that I'm here?"

Elizabeth pushed the bowl toward me. "No complaints from me."

Grace spun around on the stool. "I might complain, but only because I want to add pecans and I know you won't let me."

"No nuts in pancakes," Elizabeth insisted. "It's a crime against nature."

"Speaking of crimes, did the break-in have anything to do with the case you're working on?" Grace asked.

"I think so."

Elizabeth plugged in the griddle. "Have you narrowed down the suspects?"

"Not as much as I'd like. There are still a few more I need to interview." I whipped together the ingredients and left Elizabeth in charge of measuring out the right amount for each pancake. With Grace in charge of the ladle, we'd end up with snowman-shaped pancakes.

"We can help you brainstorm while you're here," Elizabeth offered as we ate our pancakes. "It would be fun to solve a real-life puzzle."

"That's a good idea. I'm also thinking about going out later. Any interest in coming along?"

"Apocalypse?" Grace asked. It was impossible to miss the note of eagerness in her voice.

"That's the place." Palmer had given me an idea in the basement bar. I had plenty of former contacts I could approach for help with the case. It would be good for me to get reacquainted with the world again. I'd been cloistered in Dark Hollow for far too long.

"What time?" Grace asked.

"Early enough to have a private conversation with the owners."

Grace rolled her eyes. "Oh, I see. This is actually a work excursion."

I leveled her with a look. "Do you want a cider or not?"

She hopped off the stool. "I want."

"Good. You're in charge of cleaning up the kitchen because you need the practice. I'm going to call Martin and then check on the animals."

"I guess I've drawn the short straw," Elizabeth grumbled.

"Somebody has to stay. You know that."

"We can be gone for an hour," Elizabeth said. "The house won't collapse in on itself like a dying star."

"It might if something happens to prevent us from coming back," I said. "What if the portal malfunctions or we get hurt?"

Elizabeth sulked. "I know, I know. You don't have to remind me."

Grace looked at her askance. "Since when do you want to go anywhere?"

"Never mind." Elizabeth left the room in a huff.

Isis joined me as I made my way through the house. The cat didn't want to leave my side now that I was home. I understood. It had been years since we'd spent any time apart. Our bond was stronger than the average human and cat and that made separation harder.

I sequestered myself in the study and updated Martin on the case.

"And you have no idea who attacked you?"

"No. I'm sorry."

"Don't be sorry. I'm only glad you're home safe. You know, I have an agent coming off another case. I can send him to finish the Neff case now if you're not up to it."

I tensed. "I'm not staying home, Martin. I'm regrouping. Do not send another agent to finish my case."

"I wasn't trying to offend you, Kit. I was only trying to be accommodating."

"I can handle this." I wanted to prove it to myself as much as anyone. "While I have you on the phone, what can you tell me about Palmer? You haven't answered my messages."

"Right. Palmer. Vampire from a wealthy family. Arrogant, as I recall."

"That's the one. He claims someone hired him to find Dottie's killer because they don't think we're up to the task."

"Has he impeded your progress?"

"No. As a matter of fact, he's been a strange combination of competitive and encouraging. Even helpful at times."

"I'll look into it," he said vaguely. "In the meantime, take care of yourself. If you're in danger, retreat and get help."

I smiled at the phone. "What do you think I'm doing?"

I finished the call and went outside to check on the plants and animals. As enchanted as Dark Hollow was, it still required upkeep.

I skirted the lake and spotted Elizabeth snug as a bug in a hammock. Despite the fact that her face was blocked by a book, I'd recognize the shape of her feet anywhere. Like a pair of ballet slippers, they were pale, narrow, and elegant.

"What are you reading?" I asked.

The hammock rocked once before flipping over and dumping its occupant unceremoniously on the ground.

She shot me an accusatory glance. "You frightened me."

"By walking toward you like a normal person?"

"I was reading. You know how I get."

Oh, I knew. Elizabeth could be seated right next to you, but if she was holding an open book, she was miles away. I'd repeated myself enough times over the years to recognize the significance of the dreamy expression.

Her familiar swooped down from a nearby tree branch. I didn't realize the raven was there until his feathers brushed my head on the way to the hammock. As a white raven, you wouldn't think camouflage was Edgar's strong suit, but the bird was surprisingly adept at it.

"Not to worry," I said. "Your witch is fine."

Elizabeth dusted the dirt from her knees and I helped her to her feet.

"What brings you out here?"

'Out here' was code for 'my personal space.' Each of us had a special place inside the house as well as outside. Elizabeth's inside space was, naturally, the library. Outside it was this hammock, on the edge of the forest overlooking the lake.

"I'm checking on the sanctuary."

"Everything is fine. Dark Hollow isn't going to fall apart because you're away for a few days. Grace and I are more than capable." She closed the book and handed it to her familiar. The raven grasped the book with his claws and flew back toward the house.

"I'm beginning to see that."

Elizabeth leaned against a thick tree trunk. "I'm glad you're here actually. There's something I've been wanting to discuss with you."

I held up my hands. "You and Grace have to work out your issues. I'm not getting involved."

"I'm not talking about Grace." Using her big toe, she drew a line in the dirt. "I'd like to use my magic for the greater good."

"What does that mean?"

"It means I'm wasting my talents here. There are murderers and criminals out there and Hex Support doesn't have enough talent to handle them."

"Then offer your services as an analyst to Martin. You can do that from the comfort of the library."

"But what if I want to do more?"

I arched an eyebrow. "Since when do you want to do more than live vicariously through characters in a story?"

"I've been thinking about it a lot lately, but watching you with this case has convinced me. You seem so much more animated." She paused, seeming to choose her words carefully. "More alive."

I shook my head. "No, absolutely not." I started back toward the house, taking the path alongside the lake.

Elizabeth hurried after me. "I'm thirty-three years old and I never get to go anywhere. I feel like Belle trapped in the enchanted palace of the Beast."

I whipped around to face her, arms folded. "First of all, that's your dream existence so I'm not sure why you're complaining. Second of all, who is the Beast in this comparison?"

She waved a hand toward the house. "All of it. The magic. Dark Hollow. The whole Fairfield legacy."

"You love it here."

Her gaze dropped to the dirt path. "I do, but it would be nice to be out in the world every once in a while. Have a life of my own."

Sensing a juicy conversation, Bella glided across the water toward us.

"This is a private conversation, Bella," I said in a firm tone.

The black swan moved two feet away and continued swimming in circles to stay within earshot. Clever bird.

"This place has stunted my emotional growth," Elizabeth argued. "I read books to feel like I'm alive and out in the world, but these aren't my adventures. I'm living vicariously through the stories of other people. I want to write my own story."

"We have obligations."

"We have fears."

Those, too.

"You were lucky," she continued. "You got married and had children. What if I want those things, too? Who am I going to meet inside those four walls?"

"I think you'll find about seventy-two walls in our house."

Elizabeth didn't smile. "I'm being serious."

"I know you. You always are." I studied my middle sister. She was intelligent, kind, resourceful. Why couldn't she do more?

I knew why. Because there was every chance she'd end up like James. Like our mother, too. I didn't want to visit my sister's portrait on the wall of the staircase. I wanted her right here, talking to me by the lake for the rest of our natural-born lives.

She fell in step with me and together we returned to the house. "I'm more capable than you give me credit for."

"You are incredibly capable. I don't doubt that."

Gertie bleated at us from the balcony.

I glanced up. "How on earth did you get there?" That goat had an impressive range of motion.

We entered the house and went straight to the kitchen. I was pleased to see Grace had done a decent job of cleaning up.

"You're obviously intending to ask questions about your case at the Apocalypse. Maybe these are questions *I* can answer," Elizabeth said.

"These aren't answers that can be found in a grimoire."

"Maybe you could talk to the ancestors about giving me a little more freedom. Dark Hollow isn't going to crumble. We could rotate our time away to make sure one of us is always here."

"We'd have to." Dark Hollow's existence depended on it.

"We have a portal we barely use. Why not take advantage of our gifts?" She lowered her voice. "Even Imogen and Deacon are getting more freedom than I am and they're only teenagers."

"You went to college, too," I said.

"And then straight back here afterward. Do they realize that will be their fate, too?"

I glared at her. "Not if I live forever. Besides, we aren't talking about the twins right now. We're talking about you."

"Please talk to the ancestors. You're the oldest. They're more likely to listen to you."

I exhaled a resigned breath. "I'll see what I can do."

Grace would've flung her arms around me and planted sloppy kisses all over my cheek. Restrained as ever, Elizabeth merely nodded. "Thank you."

She retreated from the kitchen and I opened the cabinet for a glass.

A familiar voice rang out from the hall. "Mom, I'm home!"

My heart leaped at the sound of my daughter's voice and I abandoned my need for a drink of water. "Imogen?"

She entered the kitchen with a smile as bright as a sunflower. "Finals finished today so I decided to come straight home."

"And miss all the end-of-year parties?" I engulfed her in a tight hug. "I'm so happy to see you."

"Is Deacon home yet?"

"No. Did he have finals, too?"

"Same days as me."

"Oh." I felt like a terrible mother for living in ignorance of my children's exam schedules. It used to be that I had every noteworthy event marked on the family calendar. Tests, recitals, parties—if it involved my children, it was on the schedule. Blue marker for Imogen and purple for Deacon.

"Did someone invoke my name?"

Deacon. My heart swelled. Both kids were home for the summer and I'd been too distracted to notice the time had come. On the one hand, it was good for me. I didn't want to spend my time staring at the calendar and waiting for them. It wasn't healthy.

I lunged for my son and hooked my arms around his neck. "You smell like chemicals."

"Sorry. I came straight from my last final in the lab. I used the portal on the edge of campus."

I kissed his cheek and stepped back for a better look. "You look older. How is that possible?" He'd only been gone nine months and I'd seen him during the holidays.

Imogen's gaze darted left to right. "Where are the aunts?"

"Somewhere in the house as usual."

"I want to show you what I bought for Auntie Grace's birthday." Imogen unwrapped a delicate gold chain with a pale pink locket attached. "I saw it in an antique store in Philadelphia and it screamed her name."

My breathing hitched. "Gods, I keep forgetting it's Grace's birthday this weekend." I still had to wrap the present I bought at Guilty Treasures.

"Write this day down, ladies and gentlemen," Deacon chimed in. "Our mother has forgotten a special occasion."

I bristled. "I haven't completely forgotten. I have her gift." In my entire adult life, I never missed a birthday, anniversary, or any other celebratory event. I even remembered the birthdays of the twins' closest friends. If I forgot Grace's special day...

"Stop it right now," Imogen said. "I can see the guilt on your face."

"Can you blame me?"

Deacon laughed. "Relax, Mom. You haven't actually missed her birthday, you know."

"Deacon should know," Imogen added. "He always waits until the last minute for everything."

I looked at my son. "You don't have a gift?"

"No, but I'll have one by the weekend."

I groaned. "That doesn't make me feel any better."

Deacon sniffed the air. "You don't have Granny's special brownies ready? I was hoping for a treat."

I faltered. "I'm sorry. I wasn't expecting either one of you today. I'll start them now."

"I'll help you," Deacon offered.

"What have you been so busy with that you forgot about Granny's brownies?" Imogen scrutinized me. "You've met someone, haven't you?" She pivoted toward the doorway where Grace now stood. "Is she seeing someone, Auntie Grace?"

My youngest sister held up her hands. "Not to my knowledge, although she has been in and out more than usual."

I sucked in a shocked breath. "Because I am working a case, not because I'm dating."

"You're working a case?" I heard the note of concern in my daughter's voice.

I winced. "I'm sorry. I meant to tell you." When it was over. "If it's any consolation, the job is temporary. One assignment as a favor to Martin and then I'm done." I made a show of dusting off my hands.

Deacon took a generous bite of an apple and chewed. "Is it dangerous?"

Imogen swatted his arm. "Of course it's dangerous. Do you think Dad died because it was a teddy bear picnic?"

"Frankly I've always thought the idea of a teddy bear picnic was terrifying," Deacon said through chunks of apple. He'd inherited his father's habit of talking with his mouth full. I managed to break a lot of his bad habits before sending him out into the world, but not that one.

"Teddy bears are adorable," Imogen argued.

"Until they see you've got honey and marmalade and whatever else bears want and they turn on you."

"Paddington is the only bear who likes marmalade," Imogen said. "You can't be afraid of a bear in a raincoat."

"You can when you don't know what's underneath." Shuddering, Deacon tossed the apple core into the trashcan. "Tell us about this case."

"I can't."

"Of course you can," he urged. "We're your children. It's a well-established fact that confidentiality doesn't extend to offspring."

I gave him a wry smile. "Did you learn this at school?"

"I'd like to hear about it," Imogen chimed in. "If for no other reason than to feel better about it. I don't want to leave for college one day and come home to an empty house the next."

Grace registered her objection. "Your mother isn't the only who lives here, you know."

Deacon's gaze swept the room. "Speaking of which, where's Auntie Elizabeth?"

I nearly said "sulking" but decided against it.

"Mom's about to make Granny's brownies," Imogen said.

"Mom will do no such thing." Grace wiggled her fingers, encouraging me to leave. "The three of us will make the brownies while your mother attends to more important matters."

I could've kissed her. "Thanks, Grace. We're going to the Apocalypse later if you'd like to join us."

"Can't. I'm meeting friends in town," Deacon said.

"Same," Imogen added.

I balked. "Your first night home and you've already made plans with other people?" I couldn't help but feel disappointed.

"Sounds like you've got 'more important matters to attend to' anyway." Deacon used air quotes to emphasize Grace's words.

"Nothing is more important than you two," I said. "Nothing."

CHAPTER FIFTEEN

I made myself presentable for the Apocalypse, as you do, and climbed the curved staircase. I stopped in front of the one portrait we avoided. I stretched my neck from side to side in an attempt to limber up before what was certain to be a stressful conversation.

I formed a connection with the portrait. The paintings sometimes acted as a mood ring, the colors and image reflective of the subject's emotions. Aunt Elodie tended to wear cheerful shades of sunrise, whereas my mother opted for jewel tones. Anastasia's frame of mind was anybody's guess.

The image stirred. The high collar of her purple dress darkened to a deep shade of black.

Terrific.

Her mouth puckered and I braced myself for the unpleasantries. "Hello, Anastasia."

The witch glowered from beneath a set of bushy eyebrows. As a child, I pictured them as two warring caterpillars, fighting for dominance of her forehead. "Well, it's about time, Katherine Isabella Nola Rose Fairfield."

"You're looking well," I said.

She ignored the compliment. "I don't hang here for my health, you know. The ancestors are here for your benefit, but do you take advantage of that? Nooo. You're too good for a helping hand. You know everything and always have, just like your mother."

I stood in silence and let the insults wash over me. Anastasia had a habit of hurling insults and accusations until they lost their luster. Only then was she ready to move on to other topics.

"You must be desperate for something if you've chosen to speak to me," she observed.

"Not desperate. It's only that you've been around longer than the others."

She folded her heavy arms against an ample bosom and regarded me. "Are you calling me old?"

"I'm calling you wise. I've met a vampire named Palmer and I'd like to know more about him."

Her dark eyes glinted. "Palmer, is it?"

"That's all I know. He claims to not have another name."

"Like Charlemagne."

I bit back a smile. "Interesting reference point."

"I've heard mention of him. Tall and mysterious vampire. Bags of money."

"How many bags?" Imogen's voice jolted me and I grabbed the banister to maintain my balance.

I turned to glare at her. "You're not supposed to eavesdrop."

"I'm curious. I want to know more about this vampire, too, especially if he's working the same case as you."

"Who told you that?" I snapped.

"Come closer, Imogen," Anastasia ordered. "I'd like a better look at you. It's been far too long."

"Imogen, go back downstairs. This conversation doesn't concern you."

"She's a Fairfield witch," Anastasia interjected. "Any conversation with the ancestors concerns her."

Imogen gave me a smug look and proceeded up the steps.

"The Palmers are an ancient vampire family," Anastasia said. "I don't know which one you're dealing with, but the ones I knew were lethal with endless resources."

Deacon appeared on the landing. "Why would he investigate a murder?"

I smacked my forehead. "This isn't a conference call."

"Seriously, though," Deacon persisted. "If he's as wealthy and deadly as you say, why would he bother investigating the murder of some old bat in Savannah, especially when the police and the FBM are already on the case? What's his motivation?"

Grace had clearly been running her mouth during the baking of brownies. I began to regret my decision to leave them to it.

"Maybe the Palmers have lost their money," Imogen suggested. "He's too proud to tell you that so he pretends."

I shook my head. "I don't think so. Everything about him reeks of money, and the people I've spoken to about him also associate him with deep pockets."

"What does it matter?" Anastasia asked.

I refocused on her. "What does what matter?"

"Whether he has money, what his motivation is. I would think you'd be more concerned with solving the case than learning about your adversary."

"He isn't my adversary."

Anastasia gave me a long look. "Oh, no? It sounds to me like he's competing with you for information in an attempt to beat you to the killer. If that's not an adversary, I don't know what is."

"Except he doesn't actually seem to be competing. We're working together—sort of." I felt dirty even saying the words. It seemed like a betrayal—a Fairfield witch teaming up with a vampire. We were powerful in our own right. We didn't need assistance from the undead.

Anastasia seemed to have the same reaction because she placed a palm flat against her chest and heaved, "Whatever next?"

"Should I fetch your smelling salts, Anastasia?" Deacon offered with a good-natured smile. Gods above, that boy could charm the spots off a leopard.

"Don't be a smart-ass," Anastasia shot back, although I caught the hint of a smile. The witch had a fondness for sarcasm. I thought of Dottie and her relationship with her relatives. Her fondness for Rufus because of his happy disposition. There were definite similarities between our families.

"I suppose it doesn't matter," I admitted. "I only want to know that I'm not setting myself up for disappointment... with the investigation," I added quickly, worried that they might assume something else entirely. I was absolutely not invested, attracted, charmed by Palmer—none of the above.

"You were the top agent in Hex Support for a reason, Mom," Imogen said. "I wouldn't worry about a rogue vampire."

"Referring to him as a rogue makes him sound more appealing."

I turned to see Grace on the staircase behind Imogen. "Why don't we include Elizabeth in this discussion so we can be certain everyone's had a vote?"

Elizabeth appeared on the landing above us with her nose buried in a book. She glanced up and yawned. "What are we voting on?"

I groaned. First Palmer. Now my family. And here I thought I'd be working as a solo agent. I should've known that would be impossible. I was destined to be part of a pack rather than a lone wolf. To be fair, it was probably a good thing. Generally wolves only broke away from their packs in order to find a mate.

I shivered at the thought of the word 'mate.' I needed to stop thinking about Palmer in those terms. This was a professional arrangement and nothing more. We needed each other. Okay, 'needed' seemed too strong.

"Mom, why is your face is so red?" Imogen asked.

My hands pressed against my cheeks. "It's too warm in here. We should open more windows and let in fresh air."

Anastasia wasn't buying it. "Is it a hot flash?" she asked with a touch too much eagerness. "I remember those. You're a Green Witch, aren't you? You should know which herbs work wonders for symptoms of menopause."

Deacon grimaced. "I don't think I need a lesson in lady problems."

"Not when you are one," Imogen shot back.

Deacon pulled a face. "Hardy har. Aren't you the comedian? Maybe you should change your major to stand-up."

Imogen squared her shoulders. "Maybe I will. The world needs more women in comedy."

I jerked toward her. "I am not paying tuition at Penn so you can tell jokes at dive bars with cigarette butts on the floor and a two-drink minimum."

Imogen raised her chin a fraction. "I thought you said you only want me to be happy. No expectations."

"No, you're paying tuition so she can come live here inside an enchanted prison," Elizabeth muttered.

I looked at Imogen. "You're not seriously thinking about a career in comedy, are you?"

She scrunched her nose. "When have I ever been funny?"

Relief washed over me. "I do only want you to be happy."

Anastasia sniffed. "Imogen is a witch. She shouldn't be

studying anything except her magical specialty. You're too permissive, Katherine. Ever since James died, you let these children dictate the terms of their lives and there's simply no point."

Imogen laughed. "No point? This isn't your century, Anastasia. Women have opportunities now."

"I'm not talking about your ability to work a drive-thru window," Anastasia snapped.

Grace pushed past me. "Nice seeing you again, Anastasia. Ta-ta for now." She waved a hand at the portrait and the ghostly witch returned to her two-dimensional form.

"I wish I could control her that easily," I grumbled.

Grace turned to face us. "You're welcome. Now, what time are we headed to the Apocalypse? I don't know about you, but I could really use a drink."

Grace and I stood in front of the oil painting in the hall. I leaned forward and placed my hands on the canvas, forming a connection to the portal.

"Apocalypse," I said.

The image changed to what was best described as a dive bar. The stools at the counter were covered in cowhide. An old jukebox glittered against the wall. Grace referred to the decor as 'apocalypse chic.'

We clasped hands and entered the bar. When the twins were seven, Deacon asked me what it felt like to walk through the portal. He was fascinated and wanted to know if it hurt.

Like do all your bones break and then reform on the other side?
No, the worst that happens is your hair gets a little mussed.
Well, that's disappointing.

I smiled at the memory. At the time Elizabeth had expressed concern that he might be a psychopath, but I knew it was only his inquisitive mind at work. She'd since arrived at the same conclusion.

Death greeted us on the other side. He co-owned the bar with his three brothers—Conquest, War, and Famine. They were surprisingly cheerful guys under the circumstances and they served excellent cider.

"As I don't live and don't breathe," Death declared at the sight of us. "Two Fairfield witches at once. What have we done to deserve this blessing?"

I sat on a stool across the counter from him as my sister went to explore the jukebox options. "Two apple ciders, please."

"It's great to see you, Kit." He leaned across the counter and kissed my cheek. "You reek of me. Where've you been hanging out recently?"

"I'm working on a murder case in Savannah."

Deep lines rippled across his brow. "I sense more than a single murder."

"There's a vampire in the mix."

"Must be one powerful vampire if I can smell him on you."

I shifted on the stool. "I don't think you smell him *on* me."

"Sorry. I didn't mean it like that." He poured the cider and set three pints on the counter.

"There's a vampire involved. He claims to have been hired by a private party, but now that I'm fully immersed in the case, I can't for the life of me think of anyone who might've hired him. It doesn't make sense."

"What's his name?"

"Palmer."

Death started to choke. "Palmer, you said?" His voice was ragged from coughing.

"Yes. I take it you've heard of him."

He laughed. "Oh, yeah. We're the Four Horsemen of the Apocalypse. Of course we've heard of Palmer."

Consider my curiosity piqued. "Why? Who is he?"

Death tossed a white cloth over his shoulder. "Do you remember how we ended up buying this place?"

"You retired and wanted a place to relax for the rest of eternity."

He pinned me with a hard look. "And how did I manage to retire?"

"You sold your organization to..." My jaw unhinged. "I don't think I ever asked." Or if he told me at the time, I didn't remember.

"I'll give you one guess."

"Palmer."

Death nodded. "You got it."

"So he's in charge of the reapers," I said, more to myself. I was trying to fit the pieces together. The cider wasn't helping. The alcohol went straight to my head.

"That guy is all about power and control. If you're in his way, he will mow you down without a second thought."

"Then why did you sell to him? You could've held out for another buyer."

He snorted. "First, the money was eye-watering. Being part of an ancient vampire family has its advantages. Second, he had the skills necessary to run a worldwide organization like The Reaper Group. Some folks have the funds but not the skills. Some have the skills but not the funds." He wiped down the counter in front of me. "Palmer had both."

It suddenly struck me that Palmer's involvement was the reason Martin was so eager for me to get there and solve the murder. He knew there was another player in the mix right from the start. Someone powerful. It was the reason he'd been dodging my questions about the vampire. Now I understood why the ghost in the graveyard had been so frightened when I'd asked about Palmer. I might as well have been asking about the devil himself. The ghost was perfectly content scaring tourists in the cemetery. He didn't want to be reaped by Palmer or anyone else.

"Thanks, that's really helpful information."

Death grinned. "No problem. Anything else I can do for you? All you have to do is ask." Another patron caught his eye at the end of the bar. "Be right back."

While Death was chatting at the opposite end of the counter, Famine and Grace joined me at the stools.

"What mischief have you two been getting up to?" I asked.

"Famine wants me to come to a party this weekend."

"I'm afraid she has plans. It's her birthday."

"Too bad. I was thinking all three of you could come," Famine said.

Grace's face fell. "That won't ever happen."

"You know my brother's always been sweet on you," Famine said. "Now that you're single..."

I shook my head. "I'd have to give up my favorite watering hole once the relationship ended. Sorry, not worth it."

Grace nudged me. "She's smitten with someone. That's the real reason."

Famine leaned forward, all ears. "Do tell."

"She's lying. There isn't anyone."

Famine wagged a finger at me. "You're blushing. Is it the vampire you mentioned to my brother? Nothing wrong with my hearing, you know."

"I hope not," Grace said. "From what Death said, Palmer sounds more dangerous than the killer you're chasing."

"Palmer isn't a threat." Not to me, anyway.

"How can you be sure?" she pressed.

"Because if he wanted to hurt me, he would've done it by now." As soon as the words left my mouth, I knew it was true.

Palmer hadn't been the one to attack me in the cemetery, not that I ever really believed it. It was a theory I was more than happy to dismiss. The only questions left unanswered were the reason for Palmer's involvement and—of course—who killed Dottie Neff?

CHAPTER SIXTEEN

I returned to Savannah the next day feeling refreshed. The short break at home was exactly what I needed. Armed with knowledge about Palmer and having the twins home for the summer, I felt ready to dive back in and solve the case.

I started with Luke and Lauren Mulgrew. The brother and sister lived in one of the historic houses on West Macon Street not far from Madison Square.

"Good morning. I'm Agent Fairfield from the Federal Bureau of Magic."

The man at the door didn't balk. "Come in, Agent Fairfield."

The interior retained its mid-nineteenth-century charm. Pale yellow walls were off-set by mahogany wood. The accent colors were red and gold, including a chaise lounge upholstered in a deep red velvet fabric. A shorter, female version of him emerged from an adjacent room.

"I'm Dr. Luke Mulgrew and this is my sister, Lauren."

Lauren nudged her brother's arm. "Everybody calls him Dr. Luke."

The resemblance was obvious. They shared the same shade of light brown hair and the same sloped nose.

"I'm here to ask a few questions about your cousin, Dottie Neff."

They exchanged apprehensive glances.

"This won't take long. I promise."

Dr. Luke checked his watch. "I don't need to be at the hospital until later, so I have time."

"I always have time," Lauren said. "I'm between jobs."

An interesting disclosure.

"Your home is lovely." A low pressure began to build at the base of my skull and I quickly brushed it aside. I had to focus.

"Thank you. The only reason we can afford it is because we pooled our money."

Dr. Luke glared at his sister. "I don't think Agent Fairfield cares about our bank statements."

"Some people think it's strange that we still live together," Lauren continued. "But Luke works such long hours at the hospital, it doesn't make sense for him to live alone and I don't have much in the way of savings."

I gave her a reassuring smile. "I don't think it's strange. I live with my sisters and my children." I opted not to mention the ancestors or the animals.

"I think it's nice when generations of family live together," Lauren said. "That's how it used to be. Modern families are too fractured."

She sounded congested, which was confirmed when she barked a wet cough. She quickly covered her mouth and apologized.

A banging sound drew my attention to the ceiling. It sounded like someone was hitting the pipes with a metal object.

"What's that noise?" I asked.

Lauren waved a dismissive hand. "Don't mind her. That's Adeline Moss. She lives with us."

"Another relative?" I asked over the din.

Dr. Luke smiled. "No, Adeline came with the house. She's a ghost."

That explained the pressure I felt.

Lauren observed me expectantly. "Does that shock you?"

"I live with half a dozen ghosts, so no."

Her eyes widened. "I feel sorry for you. Adeline is enough of a handful. I can't imagine more."

"What does she do?"

"What doesn't she do?" Lauren said.

"Open and closes doors and windows," Dr. Luke added. "Hides items where they don't belong. Leaves out our unmentionables for guests to see."

"Basically, she likes to frighten our guests, which is what this little display is." Lauren cupped her hands around her mouth and yelled, "You can knock it off, Adeline. This lady has her own ghosts at home."

The banging ceased.

"Can you see her?" I asked.

"No," Dr. Luke said. He cupped his hands around his mouth and yelled at the ceiling, "But we can hear her just fine."

"Sometimes I think it would be nice to get another job just to be out of the house more often," Lauren said. "The problem is I usually end up on disability and then as soon as my employer can let me go without legal consequences, they do."

"Why do you end up on disability?"

"I have a chronic illness." She blew her nose. "Which leaves me feeling rundown all the time and susceptible to whatever cold or flu is running amok." She coughed. "Sort of like right now."

"I'll fetch the healing stones," Dr. Luke said. He crossed the room and opened the top drawer of a mahogany highboy where he retrieved a small drawstring bag. He dumped the contents in the palm of his hand and rubbed them with his other hand.

"Are those moonstones?" I recognized the type of stone from Guilty Treasures, although these seemed bluer and smoother than the ones behind the safety glass.

"They are, indeed."

Lauren sneezed dramatically and wiped her nose with a tissue. "I have chronic allergies."

"Seasonal?"

"If that includes all the seasons, then yes." She gestured to her brother with the tissue. "Luke takes good care of me."

"I do my best," the doctor said as he rubbed a stone along her forehead. "Sometimes I question my methods, especially during times like these when they don't seem to do any good."

I mentioned a few herb alternatives. "Have you tried any of those?"

Dr. Luke shot me a quizzical look. "No, but now that you mention it, I will." He heaved a sigh. "This is the downside to straddling two worlds. I don't fully inhabit either one."

My thoughts instinctively turned to Deacon. "I understand completely. My son is a wizard studying sciences at Johns Hopkins and I worry he'll suffer the same consequences."

"I'm a Bulldog myself, but that's an excellent school."

"He seems to have enjoyed his first year, but I do worry about trying to live two disparate lives."

Dr. Luke offered a sympathetic smile. "I didn't mean to sound so negative. I'm not a particularly powerful mage. Medicine is much more useful to me." He inclined his head toward his sister. "And to Lauren."

"I prefer natural remedies," Lauren said, still sounding as stuffy as the moment I arrived. "If the stones don't work, I'll try those herbs you mentioned."

He shifted the stone to her cheeks. "These stones are family heirlooms. They were passed down from our great-uncle Frederick who was a well-known healer in the community. His mage abilities were much stronger than our generation."

"Except for Dottie," I said.

His face tightened, but he made no comment.

"That's probably why the stones don't work too well," Lauren said. "Luke's magic isn't strong enough."

"Tell me about your relationship with Dottie," I said. "Would you characterize it as positive?"

Lauren snorted. "Nobody had a positive relationship with Dottie, not even Dottie."

"I don't know about that. Her assistant seemed to get along with her, and George and Jack Barnes."

Lauren gave me a deadpan look. "Those are people she paid. I'm talking about everyone else."

Dr. Luke moved the moonstone to Lauren's throat. "My sister's right. Dottie was known as a bully in our family."

"Yet you attended her parties."

His gaze flicked to me. "Of course. I had no reason not to."

"I went for the scallops wrapped in bacon," Lauren said. "She loved to serve them as appetizers."

I didn't blame her. "You didn't decide as a group to boycott Dottie's events until she allowed Daisy back into the fold?"

They looked at each other.

"That would've been smart," Lauren said.

Dr. Luke slid the stones back into the drawstring bag. "If

Rufus wasn't willing, I don't see why we should've taken up the cause."

"You would've done it for me, though, wouldn't you?" Lauren asked. It was more of a statement than a question.

"Yes, of course."

Lauren shifted to an upright position. "And I would've done it for Luke. Rufus and Daisy are close, but Rufus always liked Dottie's attention. I think he was afraid to disappoint her."

"Let's be honest. We were all afraid to disappoint her," Dr. Luke said. "It's not as though Daisy took a stand. She was just being herself."

Lauren's eyes were downcast. "I miss Daisy. I think I've ended up avoiding her so as not to upset Dottie. You know someone would've reported seeing us together."

"You didn't want to get on Dottie's bad side," I said.

"Of course not. I didn't like her, but being on her bad side was...Well, you see how it played out for Daisy."

"And I also see how it played out for Dottie."

Lauren allowed herself a tiny smile. "Proof that karma is real."

"Proof that someone had a weapon and wasn't afraid to use it."

Dr. Luke took a renewed interest in me. "Have they identified the murder weapon? I know she was decapitated..."

Lauren hit his arm. "Don't say that."

"What? I'm stating a fact."

"Just because you're a doctor doesn't mean you can go around putting gory images in my head."

"They've identified the weapon as a blade of some kind, but they haven't located it. Can you think of anyone in attendance at the tea party with access to a sword or another type of blade?"

He snorted inelegantly. "How about everyone? This is

Savannah. We have deep roots here. If you don't have a sword on your wall, can you even call yourself a Southerner?"

My gaze swept the room. "Where's yours?"

"In the dining room," he said. "Would you like to see them?"

"Absolutely."

"Not me," Lauren said. "I don't want to imagine what one of those things might've done to Dottie." She scrunched her nose. "Nobody deserved that, not even her."

I followed Dr. Luke to the adjacent room where a mahogany table took pride of place in the room. Two crossed swords were fastened to the wall.

"Let me guess. Mother's side of the family and father's side of the family."

He chuckled. "I guess you've seen this setup before."

"I have." I moved closer to examine them. "You're sure they haven't been moved recently."

"If I'd shown up at the costume party with a sword, somebody would've questioned it. I dressed as Tweedle Dee."

"And Lauren was Tweedle Dum?"

"That's right."

"Do you recall anyone who had a blade at the party? Any kind of blade?"

"Nobody stabbed me so it's hard to be sure, although I'm fairly certain Clement brought his Mulgrew sword. He was waving it around before he was kicked out."

"Yes, I've spoken to Clement. Do you have any thoughts on who might've killed Dottie?"

Dr. Luke rubbed his face. "I've been thinking about it ever since the party, but I honestly have no idea. Beheading someone isn't easy. Whoever did it would have to be strong and skilled with a blade."

"You're both of those things," Lauren said, as though the thought had just occurred to her.

He patted her hand. "Yes, of course, but I was with you the entire time."

"Except when you went to the restroom," Lauren countered. "Remember? You told me to stay put."

Dr. Luke's face reddened. "Lauren, you're making me look guilty. Dottie was still alive when I came back from the restroom. She was arguing with Clement, remember? We commented on his poor manners."

Lauren blushed. "Oh, yes. Now I remember. Sorry, Luke. I didn't mean to suggest you'd done anything wrong."

"It's okay." He turned to me. "You see, Agent? Only innocent parties in this house."

"Would you mind if I ran a quick test on this sword?"

He retrieved the weapon from the wall. "Be my guest. Anything you see here is fair game. I'd like to see the killer brought to justice as much as anyone."

I used my Reveal concoction on the sword. Like Clement's, there was no trace of evidence.

"For what it's worth, I don't know if a sword is the weapon you should be looking for," Dr. Luke remarked. "If what they say about the statue is true, I don't see how the killer could've chopped off the head of a statue with a blade like this. It would be much more difficult than flesh and bone."

I handed the sword to the doctor. "You seem to speak from experience."

He shrugged. "A drunken prank in medical school. We stole a statue and treated it like a cadaver—or tried to." He shook his head. "Ruined a set of good tools that day. Lesson learned."

"Thanks for indulging me, Doctor." I gave him my card. "If you think of anything else, please let me know."

"No problem." He escorted me to the door as the pipes began to bang again.

"And if a vampire named Palmer comes around, you might want to mention your ghost troubles. He can probably help you with Adeline."

His eyes shone with hope. "I would like that very much. I could really use a good night's sleep."

Behind him, Lauren coughed her response. "We both could."

CHAPTER SEVENTEEN

With one cousin left to go, I wasn't feeling very optimistic. I also hadn't crossed paths with Palmer since my return to Savannah, not that I was bothered by his absence.

Nope. Not bothered at all.

I tracked Bex to a hearse parked on the street. Clement was right about his cousin—Bex was pretty. With light brown hair, expressive brown eyes, and a killer figure, she was by far the most attractive member of the mage family.

"Are you Bex?"

She glanced at me. "Yeah. Sorry, but I'm fully booked tonight. Bachelorette party." She motioned to the hearse where a group of women were climbing to stand on top of the vehicle. The roof had been rigged to accommodate them.

"I'm not here for a tour. I'm Agent Fairfield. I'd like to ask you..."

"Questions about dead Dottie. Yeah, I heard you were making the rounds." She patted the hearse. "I'm about to give a ghost tour with these drunk gals, so if you want to talk to me while I'm on the clock, you're going to have to join the party."

My gaze shifted to the roof as one of the girls leaned over and puked over the side.

Bex cringed. "Occupational hazard. I clean it up after. From the looks of them, it won't be the last time."

I climbed in and sat in the passenger seat. The bachelorettes cheered as the motor sprang to life.

"Ghosts, ghosts," they chanted and stomped on the roof. It felt like the ceiling might cave at any moment and I braced myself for impact. Champagne splashed on my window.

Bex offered a rueful smile. "Twenty-five bucks a head and they tip well." Her gaze shifted to the ceiling. "Plus the one in the red dress is hot."

"If you're down here, who's giving the tour?"

Bex lifted the microphone from the speaker system. "Welcome to Savannah's best ghost tour, ladies. I'm your tour guide, Bex. Rules are simple. No puking on the windshield. If it's too chunky, it gets caught in the wipers. Don't lean too far over the side or we might be seeing your ghost on future tours."

She slowly accelerated.

"Do you actually show them any ghosts?"

She laughed. "I'm sure I do, but none of us can see them."

"How long have you been doing this?"

"Three years. I finally paid off the hearse last month. This is a good job for me because I get to sit most of the time. I have chronic fatigue syndrome. Everyone thinks I'm lazy. In my opinion, they're too lazy to bother to understand my condition."

"You're playing to your strengths. That's smart." I cast a sidelong glance at her. "Did Dottie think you were lazy?"

Bex grunted. "Yeah. She liked to comment on my inactivity."

"That must've annoyed you."

"One second." She spoke into the microphone. "We've

reached Monterey Square. If you look to your left, you'll see the Mercer-Williams House made famous by the murder described in the novel *Midnight in the Garden of Good and Evil*." She dropped the microphone and looked at me. "Everything about Dottie annoyed me. She was an attention-seeking, money-grubbing wannabe witch who didn't appreciate how lucky she was."

"In what way?"

Bex gave me an incredulous look. "In every way. Have you seen her house? She got the magic, the money, the confidence. Everything. It's like Sleeping Beauty's christening, except the fairies give all their gifts to the firstborn and there's nothing left over for anyone else."

She eased down the street to another building. "This house has a well-known ghost that likes to pull out the owner's underwear."

An upside-down face appeared at the driver's side window. "Hey, Bex," the bachelorette shouted.

Bex rolled down the window. "Yeah, hon?"

"We want to pull over. Jasmine needs to pee."

Rolling her eyes, Bex pulled over and parked. She picked up the microphone. "There's a public restroom one block down on the left, or you can try the bushes as long as nobody sees you." She paused. "Just don't choose the rose bush. That won't end well for her."

I glanced outside as the bachelorettes climbed down from the hearse. "I thought Jasmine was the one who needed to pee."

"Doesn't matter. They always go in groups."

"Talk to me about the tea party."

"Pretty boring when I was there. The excitement happened after I left."

"Happened or was reported?"

She shrugged. "That part I don't know since I'm not the

one who killed her." She looked at me sideways. "That's why you're here, right? To decide whether I killed her?"

"That's my job."

The girls returned to the roof and Bex rejoined the street. "I didn't kill her. I don't feel as bad as I should about her death, though."

"She seems pretty unpopular for a woman who drew record numbers to her parties."

"I went for the free booze and the gossip." She slowed the hearse and reached for the microphone. "Check out this cool statue. Can anybody guess who it is?"

"So you can't see ghosts either?" I asked.

"Most of my magic is directed toward living a normal life and sustaining my energy levels. There isn't much left over for anything else."

"You talk as though it's a finite resource."

"No, but it's like any other kind of energy. It needs to be replenished and I'm not always in a condition to do that. I sleep a lot, but rest alone isn't enough."

"I'm sorry. That must be difficult for you."

"I manage."

She took a turn too sharply and screams from above nearly shattered my eardrums.

"Oops." She rolled down the window and yelled, "Sorry!"

"Did you interact with Dottie at the party?"

"Of course. I have manners. I said hello. Didn't find her by the time I left. I told Rufus to give her my regards. She might actually buy it coming from Mr. Smiley."

"What was your costume?"

"I wanted to be Tweedle Dee, but Luke and Lauren stole that idea. I went as an Ace of Spades. Made sitting down a little awkward. I had the bottom of a card jammed up my butt half the time."

"Did you notice anything out of the ordinary at the party?"

"They ran out of mimosas pretty quickly, which I resented. Otherwise, no."

"Did you recognize everyone there?"

"Hard to tell when we were all in costume, but I saw all my cousins except Daisy. Mandy was there, of course. She's very cute in that girl-next-door way, albeit a little immature for me. George was there. He was on point dressed as one of the queen's guards. It's one of the few times he gave off uncle energy instead of dad vibes." She laughed. "Must've been the spiked sweet tea."

A thought occurred to me. "Was he carrying a sword by any chance?"

"Not that I recall, but there were a few costumes with them so it wouldn't have seemed out of place."

I wasn't aware of any motive the lawyer would have for killing off his coveted client anyway.

We stopped in front of a grey building a block from the river.

"Pirates' House," Bex announced. "Bloodthirsty pirates have haunted this former inn since 1753."

"Ooh, pirates are so hot," one of the girls declared.

A spiked heel tapped the window and I lowered the glass. "Yes?"

"Like, will we see Johnny Depp here?" a voice called.

I rolled up the window without answering.

Bex glanced at me. "See any ghosts? Might be fun to liven things up for these ladies."

I scanned the area. "Not at the moment. They're probably inside the building."

The bride climbed down from the top of the hearse and knocked on the driver's window.

Bex rolled it down. "Another bathroom break?"

"Can we go inside for a drink? We're out of champagne."

"Sure," Bex said. "I recommend the rum flight."

The drunk bride booped Bex on the nose. "Thanks, hon. You're the best." She cupped her hands around her mouth and summoned her own band of pirates. The hearse rocked from side to side as the other members of the party made their way to the ground.

"I might go in for a Shirley Temple," Bex said. "See if I can make headway with the hot one."

"In that case, I'll make my way back from here."

"You have any more questions before I go?" she asked.

"No, but if you think of anything, will you let me know?" I gave her my card.

"I doubt I will, but sure."

We exited the hearse and Bex locked the doors.

"I hope you find whoever killed Dottie. I won't be shedding any tears over it, but I won't go dancing on her grave either."

Fair enough.

Leaning against the hearse, I watched Bex as she sauntered behind the group of drunken bachelorettes.

"Looks like you've had a fun evening."

I turned to see the vampire on the sidewalk illuminated by a streetlight. "Fun for them maybe."

"I feel like I missed an opportunity there. This cousin is pretty."

"Save it, Palmer. She's not your type."

He straightened his lapels. "You can't be serious. I'm everyone's type."

"She's a lesbian."

He gazed in the direction of Bex. "How could you tell?"

"Because of the two small horns on her head." I smacked his arm. "Because she was hitting on one of the girls, ignoramus."

Grinning at me, he rubbed his arm. "Humor and spunk. You know, Ms. Fairfield, you're beginning to grow on me."

"Agent Fairfield."

"So you keep telling me, yet in the same breath you've told me this is a temporary assignment."

"And in your same breath you said you were hired by a private party to conduct your own investigation, but that isn't true, is it?"

He slid his hands into his trouser pockets. "I've been discovered, have I?"

"Yes, Mr. Death, you have. Why don't you tell me the whole story?"

He gestured in the direction of the riverfront. "It's a lovely evening. Let's take a stroll."

Moonlight rippled across the river as we walked side by side.

"How much do you know?" he asked.

I repeated what Death told me at the Apocalypse.

"I should have known your network would extend beyond the realm. I'm here to find Dottie Neff."

"Her ghost."

"Her shade," he corrected me. "She never made it to the crossroads, which means she's still here. I fired the reaper for his incompetence. I haven't had time to find a replacement yet and I enjoy Savannah, so I decided to come on my own and handle it personally."

"And you thought working the case alongside me might lead you to her?"

"To wherever her shade is hiding, yes."

I stared at him in disbelief. "I can see ghosts. If she were here, I would know."

"Not if she doesn't want you to. If she thinks we're together, she won't want to make herself known to you."

"Why wouldn't she at least show herself and tell us what happened? She'd want her killer brought to justice."

"Because she doesn't want to cross over more than she wants her killer caught. Trust me, I've seen it enough times to know. She's hiding somewhere. She probably hopes I'll get bored and give up. Decide one shade isn't worth the effort. It happens. That's why you have shades—or ghosts—in the first place."

"How do you know she's here? Maybe she's hiding somewhere in Paris by now." I pictured Dottie, the afterlife of a Parisienne ghost party.

The vampire shook his head. "She can't leave. That's not how it works."

I thought of our afterlife attachment to Dark Hollow. "Explain it to me."

"The farthest she might be able to go is the Florida border, or South Carolina."

"The afterlife adheres to geopolitical boundaries? Interesting."

"It's the way it's set up. If the border changes, our border changes along with it. This makes life easier for our reapers, although most of the time, the soul doesn't want to travel too far from their place of death anyway, unless they died somewhere unusual."

"So you think Dottie is lurking somewhere in Savannah?"

"I'm certain of it. You can see shades, too. I thought you were the ideal companion for this venture."

I frowned. "Then you don't even care who killed her. You only want to capture her."

"On the contrary, I care, but justice isn't my top priority. The natural order is."

I clasped my hands behind my back. "So you're like a mob boss."

"How am I like a mob boss? The people I deal with are already dead."

"But you dispose of them. Make sure that they're disposed of."

"Then you might as well call me a trash collector, but I don't like viewing people as trash, do you?"

"Why did you act like you were competing with me if you don't actually care who the killer is?"

"Because I thought it might spur you on to solve the case more quickly. Your file suggests you're high competition."

"I haven't been competitive in a long time. I've had other priorities. Why did you buy the organization from Death?"

"Because he was selling it. Next question."

"Why did you want to run a global reaper organization?"

"It's lucrative. I have the requisite skills." His brow furrowed. "Does it matter?"

"I don't know why someone would be drawn to that kind of business. It makes sense for someone like Death."

"I'm a vampire. You don't think the business of the dead makes sense for me?"

"Do you personally oversee all your employees? Seems like you need to learn to delegate responsibility."

"Like our dearly departed Dottie, I do like a certain level of power and control."

"The highest level."

He inclined his head in acknowledgement. "You'd make an excellent reaper. Any interest in jumping to a new line of work?"

"I'm a witch."

"And? We have witches on the payroll. Mages. Even other vampires. As long as you possess the right skill set, you're considered a contender."

"I don't think a job as a reaper would suit me but thanks

for the compliment." I glanced at him out of the corner of my eye. "Anything else to add or is that the whole story?"

"Not quite." His mouth twitched. "I wasn't expecting to enjoy your company as much as I have. Another reaper became available, but I told him I intended to see this case through. There. Now you have the whole story."

Warmth spread through my body. "You stayed in Savannah because of me?"

"Well, for the shade of Dottie Neff, but also for you." His arm brushed against mine. "This is the part where you insult me or tell me to...suck it."

"I'm flattered, Palmer, but I'm not in the market for a relationship."

"You've been alone for ten years, Ms. Fairfield. Don't you think you've punished yourself long enough?"

I shot him a quizzical look. "What makes you think it's punishment?"

"To deprive yourself of the company of the opposite sex..."

"I have a son."

The vampire gave me a pointed look. "You know what I mean." He stopped walking and turned to face me. "How about this? Once this case has been resolved, you and I will have a proper date. Dinner, drinks, the works."

I arched an eyebrow. "Define 'the works.'"

"I'll leave it to your imagination."

I hesitated. "I'll consider your offer."

"No pressure."

A breeze rushed past us and my skin tingled. Elizabeth had been right about me. I felt more alive than I had in a decade.

"Why don't we concentrate on the case for now?"

"I thought you might say that. It's ironic Dottie was the only one with enough magic to see shades."

"Daisy mentioned catching a glimpse of her, but then thought she might've imagined it."

"Could she have been mistaken?"

"I don't know. Daisy is supposedly the weakest of the cousins, although, to be fair, they're all pretty weak compared to Dottie."

"Where to now? The Springhouse?"

"No, I'm not staying there, not after the break-in."

"If you need a place…"

I smiled. "No, thank you."

"I was simply going to recommend a charming inn in the historic district. Excellent service. Very attentive."

"I'll keep it in mind for next time."

I turned and walked away. I was determined to wrap up this case in order to join the family for Grace's birthday at Dark Hollow.

Grace's birthday.

I thought of her gift, still unwrapped in my bedroom, as well as the charmed jewelry in Guilty Treasures, like the necklace I wore to the Spring Fling. What if Dottie had owned a charmed ring or necklace—a piece of jewelry that had been coveted by the killer? A Mulgrew family heirloom that Dottie had refused to share.

I thought of the healing stones Dr. Luke had been using to help Lauren. He'd mentioned they were family heirlooms. What if they'd belonged to Dottie and he'd taken them?

There was one way to find out.

I swiped my phone from my handbag. "Hello, Mr. Mahon. This is Agent Fairfield. Would you mind if I come by your office? There's something I'd like to see."

CHAPTER EIGHTEEN

I sat across from George Mahon and closed the file on the desk. "There's no mention of healing stones in the will."

"Were you expecting to see them?"

"I was hoping." If they were that special, they would've been singled out. "Do you recall Dottie mentioning them or seeing any at her house?" I described the ones I'd seen at Dr. Luke's house.

"Not offhand, but there's an inventory list if you'd like to see that. We attached it as an addendum to the will. It's referenced in paragraph 3(b)."

I must've skimmed right over it. Not a surprise, really. The will made for some dense reading. "That would be great, thanks."

"Mandy updated the list a couple months ago. There are a few missing items which Dottie disposed of prior to her death, including the heirloom bequeathed to Percival, but Mandy only conducted inventory with Dottie twice a year so that's to be expected."

"They sound like they were very organized."

"Oh, they were. Made my job a whole lot easier." He

clicked his mouse and I heard the whirr of a printer behind him.

"Mandy thinks Dottie gave the heirloom to someone else?"

"We both think it might've been Dottie's idea of a prank. No point in letting death stop her from busting somebody's chops. Poor Percival. He's so disappointed."

He swiveled in his chair and reached for the sheets of paper. "Have fun with this."

"Thank you." I accepted the pages and immediately scanned the list for the stones. Still no mention of healing stones.

My gaze landed on another item. "I'm sorry. When did you say this list was made?"

"A couple months ago. Why?"

"No reason." My mind raced through the possibilities. "George, did Dottie ever talk to you about her family history?"

He angled his head. "How do you mean?"

"The Mulgrew mages seem to have only one powerhouse in each generation."

"That's right. And in this one it was Dottie."

"Did she ever explain the details of that? It's natural for power to be distributed and weaken over generations, or for the bloodline to remain strong like mine. It's highly unusual, however, for each generation to have most of the remaining power concentrated in a single person."

"Are you suggesting the Mulgrew family was cursed?"

I shook my head. "Not quite. I'm thinking more of an amplification charm."

George settled back against his leather chair. "I'm not familiar with that."

"It's when the original owner infuses an object with a spell designed to enhance their magic. I have a feeling that none of the Mulgrew mages were strong. It's just that only one could have possession of the amplification charm at a time." Similar to the way one living Fairfield had to remain at Dark Hollow to fuel the enchantment. "If I'm right, the object became a family heirloom, passed from one Mulgrew to the next. Dottie was the lucky recipient. It tends to work best when the person using it has a blood relation to the creator. The lock and key fit together smoothly, if that makes sense."

George nodded. "It does." He pointed to the pages in my hand. "And you see an amplification object on that list?"

"I see a possibility, and it's listed as missing. I think it might be the reason Dottie was killed."

"Then we need to figure out who has the object, so we can identify Dottie's killer."

Slowly I glanced up from the paper. "There's no need, George. I already have."

I hurried out of George's office, insisting that he reveal our conversation to no one until he heard from me.

I'd originally believed the killer had to be a certain personality type. After all, it wasn't every killer who would take the time to knock off a statue's head and replace it with his victim's.

But what if I was wrong about that part, as Palmer had suggested? What did that leave me with? Not a sadist or someone trying to send a message. Not a hired killer.

A discontented cousin.

I made my way to a neighborhood outside the city center and knocked on the door of a red brick house. The door opened and its sole occupant balked at the sight of me.

"Hello again, Mr. Mulgrew. May I come in?"

Hesitation glimmered in his eyes. Eventually Rufus

widened the gap. "Of course. Does this mean you've caught the killer?"

I crossed the threshold and he closed the door behind me. "Almost. I just have a few more questions if you don't mind. I like to be thorough."

His head bobbed. "Absolutely. Anything." He flashed that face-changing smile. The one that earned him a reputation for being happy. But my instinct had been right about Rufus. He wasn't very happy at all.

"Why did you attend the tea party?"

He looked at me with uncertainty. "Because I was invited."

"You're so close with Daisy. Why not refuse in solidarity with her?"

"I think I told you I'd originally intended to. That's why my costume was a last minute decision. But Daisy insisted that I go. She didn't want to deprive me of the chance to hang out with our other cousins."

My gaze drifted to the mantel. "Tell me, Mr. Mulgrew, did you steal the bonsai tree from the party before or after you killed Dottie?"

His head swiveled to the mantel. "I don't know what you mean. Dottie gave that to me as a gift."

"You moved in here a year ago. As of a couple months ago, that bonsai tree was still in Dottie's house and listed as part of the estate's inventory. It was marked as missing after she died, when Mandy catalogued items for the reading of the will. It's the reason you attacked me in the cemetery and then went searching for my notebook. You were concerned I'd made a note of it when I first visited your house and would put the pieces together."

"I don't know what you're talking about," he stuttered.

"Oh, I think you do. You knew that Dottie was going to show off her magic at that party, which meant she'd have the amplification charm with her. It's an awkward object to carry around, so she'd have to leave it somewhere out of sight, which would be ideal for you. I believe she left it in the shrubbery of the courtyard."

His face tightened. There was no trace of that trademark smile.

"So what happened?" I pressed. "You asked for it and she refused? I suppose you weren't accustomed to hearing no from doting Dottie."

His veneer cracked. "She caught me red-handed trying to take it from the courtyard. Tried to punish me with magic, but I was too fast for her."

"Your prop sword was that sharp?"

His gaze dropped to the floor. "I couldn't find the prop sword and I was already late. I grabbed the Mulgrew sword from the wall."

I glanced at the empty spot above the mantel. "I saw one at Dr. Luke's house. You all have one?"

He nodded. "The men do. It wasn't like I intended to use it. It just happened."

"Where is it now?"

"I threw it in the river. Didn't want any evidence."

"Off with her head," I said quietly.

He nodded somberly. "The queen is dead." He rubbed the back of his neck. "I acted in self-defense. The heat of the moment. If she hadn't tried to use magic, I wouldn't have struck her."

"It was a clean cut."

"Years of fencing lessons, remember?"

"Lessons that Dottie paid for ironically enough."

His face darkened. "Like I said, it was instinct. One minute we were at a standoff and she was calling me a huge disappointment. The next minute, her head was on the floor." He shuddered.

"Why would you mount her head on a statue if you acted in the heat of the moment? What were you trying to prove?"

He tipped his head back and sighed. "It was that stupid bird. Somebody let it out of the cage. It took her head." He grimaced at the memory. "I didn't have the stomach to chase after it."

I'd bet good money the statue of Winter had already been broken before the party, probably by Icarus and his powerful beak. The Mad Hatter had seen an opportunity to get compensation for his already-damaged property and seized it.

"The heirloom is that important to you?"

His eyes blazed with fury and indignation. "You have no idea what it's been like for me. Oldest cousin but a bastard so I don't get Dottie's legitimacy. I don't inherit Clement's muscles so I've got to work for them. To find out Dottie's magic should've been mine..." He jammed a finger in the direction of the mantel. "I deserved that bonsai tree. It was mine and she had no right to keep it from me."

"She rightfully inherited it, Rufus. She didn't steal it. If you want to be angry, be angry with the person who left it to her instead of you."

"She didn't even plan to leave it to me. I was supposed to be her favorite. She planned to leave it to Percival because he was the next *legitimate cousin*. Why on earth would a mage so shy he lives on an island need to amplify his magic?" He gave the sides of his hair a desperate tug. "Dottie was a tyrant who terrorized our family for long enough. It was time for a regime change."

"I don't think the court will see it your way."

Malice glinted in his eyes. "I'm not too worried. Don't forget. I still have the amplifier. As I said before, I like to keep it in the room where I spend the most time."

Rufus launched himself at me.

I'd like to say I easily sidestepped his attack, but I

wasn't nimble enough on my feet for that. Not anymore. As
I turned aside, his left side slammed into my right and
down we went. He landed on me and I slammed onto my
back. I felt the muscles scream in protest as they moved in
unnatural directions. Maybe yoga wasn't such a bad idea
after all.

It was times like this I wished my other abilities were as
strong as my Green Witch magic. Like the rest of the
Mulgrew cousins, I'd have to play the hand I was dealt.

I managed to shove him off me and scrambled to my feet.
Rushing forward, I tried to reach the bonsai tree. It was
small, but it was also hard and full of sharp edges.

Rufus grabbed the back of my shirt and I heard the tear
of the fabric. My hand shot out and my fingertips touched
the pink stones.

This time he yanked my hair and my head jerked back-
ward. I swiped the air and this time my hand brushed one of
the delicate stone leaves. Not close enough.

Rufus used his body weight to slam me against the wall.
My cheek hit the mantel of the fireplace and a searing pain
followed. That was going to bruise.

My gaze snagged on the alligator pepper plant on the
mantel. The housewarming gift from Daisy. Thanks to her
green thumb, it was in good shape. It wasn't large, but it was
enough.

Still dizzy, I whirled around to face him.

"There's something I neglected to mention about this
pepper plant."

"It's ugly?"

"Its symbolic meaning is 'judge.' It was believed to deter-
mine guilt."

He sneered. "In that case, I don't think it works too well."

"No, that part is folklore, but you were right about one
thing—it does grant wishes. You just have to know how to

access them." Pulling the plant from the pot, I cupped it in my hands and made a wish.

Rufus advanced toward me. A bright purple vein throbbed on his forehead. He grabbed me by the neck and squeezed.

I kept hold of the plant. As quickly as my fingers could move, I tore the leaves into four pieces and tossed them in four directions. I started with north, then east, south, and west.

I could scarcely breathe, but I had to say the words.

To his credit, Rufus didn't smile. He didn't seem to take pleasure in hurting me, not that it mattered.

It took all my effort to speak. "I wish you would freeze." Even as a whisper, my voice sounded hoarse.

His eyes were the last part of him to stop moving. I pried his fingers from my neck, careful not to break them in the process, and slipped out from between Rufus and the wall.

As I fumbled to retrieve my phone, the front door flew open and a familiar figure strode into the room.

"It's Rufus," Palmer announced with an air of authority. "He murdered Dottie." The vampire ground to a halt when he realized Rufus wasn't moving.

I rubbed my sore neck. "I'm a few steps ahead of you, Just Palmer."

The vampire approached the frozen mage with caution. "What did you do to him?"

"I made a wish."

His mouth quirked. "You found yourself a genie, did you?"

"Not quite. I had a little help from Mother Nature."

He spotted the remains of the plant on the floor. "Usually hitting someone with a potted plant renders them unconscious."

I tapped the phone to call Martin. "How did you figure out it was Rufus?"

"I may have eavesdropped outside George's office." He

tugged his earlobe. "Vampire hearing, remember?" He gave me an admiring glance. "Hats off to you, Ms. Fairfield. Well done."

I felt a rush of pride. It had been ten years since I'd solved a case. Ten years since I'd been anyone except sister or mother.

It felt amazing.

"If you knew, why did you let me come here alone?"

"Because I knew you could handle it. Why else?"

I frowned. "Have you been outside this whole time listening?"

"I may have entered when I heard a scuffle."

"Were you distracted—because we were scuffling for a good five minutes?"

"A neighbor stopped to talk to me. A blonde with an adorable dog named Pippa. She wouldn't stop sniffing me."

I rolled my eyes.

"What? I can't help it if I attract the females of all species."

Martin's team arrived within minutes. Either they'd been lurking within the city limits awaiting a break in the case or I wasn't the only one with a portal. Two agents carried a frozen Rufus from the house while a third bagged the sword and the bonsai tree as evidence.

"How about we meet for a drink tonight, Ms. Fairfield? I'd love to review the details with you. Perhaps we can locate Dottie together."

My phone pinged with a text from Martin requesting a full report by tomorrow. Saved by the bell.

"I would love to, except I have a report due first thing in the morning. You know how the FBM loves its bureaucracy."

"One of the reasons my firm is a private venture. I loathe red tape."

"That's the privileged part of you. You want that Oompa Loompa and you want it now."

He chuckled. "Are you comparing me to a spoiled brat?"

I shrugged. "If the stomping shoe fits."

He extended a hand. "It's been a pleasure working with you, Ms. Fairfield. It's been quite some time since I've felt like I've met someone as capable as I am."

I released his hand. "I wish I could say the same." Zing!

"Come now, you have to admit this was fun. The investigation would've been far more boring without a bit of sport mixed in."

"Well, I'm afraid your next case of a lost soul will have to go back to its usual monotony because this is my one and only case."

"More's the pity. I would've enjoyed another bout of healthy competition."

"What are the odds my next case would involve one of your missing shades anyway?"

"You'd be surprised how often it happens. And I have the means to travel anywhere I wish, much like you I imagine."

I highly doubted the vampire possessed a magic portal. Those were few and far between and typically in the hands of magic users. His method was more likely via private jet—or yacht. Maybe both.

"As enjoyable as this experience was, I'm not sure I'm ready to jump back in. I did it as a favor to Martin."

"Why would you hang up your wand after such an exhilarating experience here in Savannah?"

"I retired ten years ago. I don't see the need to retread the same path."

He grinned. "Are you sure about that? It seems to me you rather enjoyed yourself, when you weren't in mortal danger."

"It isn't as simple as what I want." The words slipped out

before I could stop them. Palmer seemed to have that effect on me.

He edged closer until I could feel his breath on the bare curve of my neck. "And why not? You're an adult. Your needs are important."

"You know what I really need right now?"

His gaze radiated heat. "I'm all ears."

"To find Dottie so you can reap her soul. Let her find peace at last."

The heat extinguished. "If you have any ideas on where to look..."

"As a matter of fact, I do."

We traveled by boat to Jekyll Island. This one was controlled by Palmer instead of skeletons.

"How did you know?" he asked as he docked the boat.

Daisy's words came flooding back to me. *I've always had good observational skills. Everyone assumes the opposite when they view you as flaky and inconsequential.*

"Daisy mentioned seeing Dottie's ghost, but she dismissed it as her imagination since no one else mentioned seeing her." It seemed that Daisy had underestimated herself. It made sense, though, that Dottie would want to apologize to the one person she'd truly wronged.

"Except Daisy couldn't hear her."

"Exactly." Although Daisy was a mage, her magic was too weak to allow her to communicate with ghosts. "Dottie probably realized then the cruel irony of being the strongest Mulgrew."

"Dottie knew the island because of Percival, and she came here to hide in plain sight until the search for her blew over. I think I felt her presence in his house when I was there."

Palmer stood on the beach and faced the island. "Yes, but hide where?"

"Follow me and I'll show you." I smiled over my shoulder at him. "You've already proven you're good at that."

We approached the former Jekyll Island Clubhouse. It was a beautifully renovated building with a tower and a huge courtyard. Families played croquet on the expansive green lawn.

Palmer looked at me askance. "You think Dottie is staying at a resort?"

"Not staying like a vacationer. Percival mentioned this is the most populated place on the island and we know that Dottie loves a crowd. She wants to hide, but she doesn't want to be alone."

"She's a ghost. I would think it's rather easy for her."

I gave him a pointed look. "In a city full of supernaturals?" I shook my head. "She knew someone was bound to spot her, especially after she showed herself to Daisy. She worried that word would get around, so she came here."

His gaze swept the area. "You're sure?"

"No, but it's a solid hunch."

We entered the lobby and it was there that I spotted an apparition that fit the victim's description. Thankfully her head was intact. Our gazes locked and her eyes registered surprise. Then she spotted Palmer. The shade turned and ran —or floated—in the opposite direction.

"I saw her. This way." I hurried through an exit door that emptied into a breezeway. I looked left then right. There was no sign of her or anyone else. There were, however, a few pillars and tall bushes to obscure my view.

Palmer squinted. "She's faster than I expected."

I had a hunch she didn't go far. "Dottie Neff, I'm Agent Fairfield with the Federal Bureau of Magic. I've been investigating your murder and I'd very much like to speak with you."

I watched and waited. The only sound was the whirr of paddle fans above our heads.

Finally, a voice said, "I know who you are. I overheard your conversation when you went to see Percival."

I shot Palmer a triumphant look.

"I visit him on occasion, when I tire of the company of strangers. Too bad his magic is too weak to see me."

"Would you show yourself? My companion and I would like to help you."

She cut me off with a grunt. "I know who your companion is, and I don't think 'help' is the word I'd choose. Under any other circumstances, I'd be thrilled to have a handsome vampire chasing after me, but not this one."

Palmer took a step forward. "Miss Neff, I understand your hesitation, but you don't want to spend an eternity hiding on Jekyll Island."

"Why not? The homes are beautiful. I'm surrounded by water. It's perfect."

"You'll be alone here."

"I'm far from alone. The resort is busy enough and Percival is here. I've managed a few pranks on the guests, and that's kept me entertained."

"Percival can't see you and neither can most of the guests," I pointed out. "You'll hate this in another month."

There was a long pause. "Are you kidding? I hate it already. I thrive on social energy and there's no one to interact with. How many times can I scare the seagulls? I mean, they deserve it. They're pests with wings, but still."

The ghost emerged from behind a pillar to my left.

"We caught Rufus," I told her. "Thought you'd want to know."

She nodded. "I wanted to talk to you, tell you what happened..."

"But you knew if you revealed yourself, then I'd tell Palmer."

Her gaze flicked to the vampire. "I didn't want to leave yet. I wasn't ready."

"Few people are." The vampire extended a hand. "Will you come voluntarily now? I have other means, but I'd rather not resort to any of them."

"I guess I'll have to be content with being the life of the afterparty." The ghost approached him with caution. "What happens next?"

"You'll come with me. After that, it'll be your secret. The truth is, I don't really know."

Her eyes rounded. "I'll know something that none of the other Mulgrews know. I'll be the first of the cousins to learn the secret." This new mindset seemed to sit well with her and she took his hand. "I'll make a deal with you. I'll come with you if we can make a quick stop in Savannah first. I owe someone an apology and I need you to communicate it for me."

I smiled. "We thought you might say that. You'll be pleased to learn that Daisy's waiting for you at her house."

Dottie squared her translucent shoulders and jutted her chin. "Then what are we waiting for? Let's go."

CHAPTER NINETEEN

Now that I was safe and sound at Dark Hollow, I felt obliged to speak on behalf of Elizabeth. Grace, too. I was the eldest and it was my responsibility to advocate for all of us.

I went to the staircase to consult the ancestors. This time I decided to start with our mother. She would understand my reluctance more than most.

I squared myself in front of her portrait and opened the lines of communication. My mother's image shifted. Her red hair rolled past her shoulders in soft waves. I never realized how much Elizabeth resembled her until this moment.

"Hi, Mom."

"Kit, what a nice surprise."

Thankfully my mother wasn't one to guilt her children for not calling enough.

"I like that top. It's a good color for you."

"Thanks." I glanced down to see a turquoise top with a V-neck. I had no recollection of choosing this shirt. It was usually whichever item was within reach. Fashion wasn't a priority for me. That was more Grace's dominion.

"How's the assignment?" my mother asked.

"Over. Elizabeth helped me," I said, testing the waters.

Her eyebrows inched up her forehead. "Your sister helped you solve a murder?"

"From the comfort of Dark Hollow, of course."

My mother examined me closely. "Is that why you've contacted me? To talk about Elizabeth?"

She'd always been perceptive. "As a matter of fact, yes."

Her face flickered with concern. "Is she sick? Is something wrong?"

"She's not sick. This is about her future." I paused. "More like her present, I guess. She'd like to spend more time away from Dark Hollow."

"Who would want that? This estate is a paradise on earth."

"It is. I agree, but sometimes it's good to take a break, even from paradise."

My mother regarded me. "You know that isn't possible."

"It is possible. It's just that we take more precautions."

"Since I died, yes. You can say it, darling. We all know I'm dead."

"The house has you and the other ancestors to sustain it."

"And it requires someone living, too."

"I know. As long as one of us is here as an anchor, why can't the other two..." I nearly said 'have a life' but changed quickly to "have their own adventures?"

"Dark Hollow requires a powerful connection to magic in order to operate. I'm sorry I can't be there in the flesh to carry that burden for you girls." Her expression softened. "You have no idea how sorry."

"It isn't a burden, Mom. We love this house."

She offered a small smile. "Why not give it a try then? Rotate one at a time. If Elizabeth is off somewhere, then you and Grace are here to hold down the fort."

I nodded. "I can make that work." I had to give my sisters

the same opportunity I was giving myself. I owed them that much.

"Kit, dinner's ready," Grace yelled.

My mother's eyes rounded. "Grace made dinner?"

I shrugged. "A lot of things are changing."

She pressed her palms to her cheeks. "My little girls are growing up."

I smiled. Only a mother would look at her forty-four-year-old daughter and say that.

I joined my family at the large table in the dining room and surveyed the faces at the table. Elizabeth. Grace. Imogen. Deacon. My heart wasn't in my body. It was right here in this room.

Grace was thrilled to open her birthday presents and seemed particularly touched by the one I'd purchased from Guilty Treasures.

"Kit, you've shocked me. Truly." Grace stared at the set of enchanted pots and pans. "I never thought you'd encourage my nonsense."

"These pots and pans will help you conduct your experiments in a neater fashion. If you want to separate certain ingredients, you tell the pan and it does it for you."

Grace clutched a small pot to her chest. "I think this is the best gift you've ever given me. It's like freedom to be myself."

Emotions clogged my throat.

"One case and you're treating us like adults," Grace remarked. "I wasn't sure how I felt when Martin first showed up, but I'm really glad about it now."

"Tell us what happened in Savannah," Elizabeth urged. "You've been very quiet about it."

"I guess I've still been processing it all."

I recounted the events of earlier this week, including the confrontation with Rufus. I omitted any references to

Palmer, however. My kids didn't need to hear about the vampire's flirtation with me.

"I don't know. The whole thing sounds dangerous," Imogen said, although she didn't sound concerned.

"Maybe so, but it sounds like you enjoyed it." Elizabeth snuck a peek at me. "A little bit, anyway."

"You're so lucky," Grace added. "Nothing interesting ever happens around here."

I laughed. "How can you say that? We live in an enchanted house and we have acres filled with magical animals."

Grace chewed thoughtfully on a carrot. "I know, but I want to use my magic the way you did. What's the point of being a powerful Chaos Witch if I only use my magic as a sprinkler for the lawn or to gather up leaves in the fall? I'm nothing but a glorified landscaper."

"You should practice being more organized," Elizabeth said. "That would be a worthwhile skill."

"Dottie's assistant is organized and look how things panned out for her," Grace pointed out. "No thanks. I'll stick to chaos."

Elizabeth's gaze flickered to me. "What do you think will happen to Mandy? Do you know if she moved in with her sister?"

"According to George, the victim's lawyer, Mandy's allowed to carry on in the guest cottage for now and the remaining cousins have agreed to move into Magnolia Hall together. One big, happy family."

Grace beamed. "Like us."

"Yes, I suppose so." I was happy for the Mulgrews. They'd suffered through this tragedy, but it would strengthen their bond. Even in death, Dottie was the unlikely glue that kept the family together.

"I wish we had cousins we were close to," Grace said.

"We do," Elizabeth pointed out. "They're just attached to portraits." She nodded in the direction of the spiral staircase.

Grace speared a carrot. "I wish we had *living* cousins we were close to. New places to visit and explore."

A bleating sound drew my attention to the doorway.

"Gertie?" I craned my neck to see the goat standing there. "How did you get in here?"

The goat bleated again in response.

"She's hungry," Grace said.

"She lives in a perpetual state of hunger," Deacon shot back. He tossed a carrot stick over his shoulder and the goat caught it mid-air.

"Please don't feed the animals at the table," I admonished him. "You know better. Gertie, go outside."

Isis appeared from a shadowy corner of the room and chased after the goat. Gertie turned and trotted out of the room.

"Please pass the salt," Grace said.

"You don't need salt. You haven't even tasted your food yet," Elizabeth scolded.

Grace made a show of lifting a forkful of chicken to her mouth and licking it. "Needs salt."

Pursing her lips, Elizabeth begrudgingly relinquished the salt shaker. "Use it sparingly. Too much salt isn't healthy."

Grace arched an eyebrow. "Neither is keeping a stick up your butt, but you seem to manage."

My phone buzzed and I glanced at the screen.

"No phones at the table," Imogen said.

"I'm not using it."

Deacon leaned over to look at the screen. "Who's Palmer?"

I snatched the phone and flipped it over.

"Why is he asking you about dinner?" Deacon asked. "Are you going on a date with someone?"

"She's an adult," Elizabeth said. "If she wants to date this vampire, why shouldn't she?"

"Vampire?" the twins echoed at the same time.

"He's the head of a grim reaper organization," Grace chimed in. She flashed a smile so devilish, she would've made Palmer proud.

"My personal life is my business, thank you very much."

"It ceased to be private when you left your phone on the table for all to see," Deacon argued.

The grandmother clock chimed twice.

Saved by the bell. I swiped my phone from the table.

"But it's dinnertime," Grace said, disgruntled.

"Our visitor clearly doesn't know that."

My chair slid back and I walked to the front door. Dark Hollow had already admitted my guest.

"There you are, my dear. Safe and sound, as I knew you would be."

"Hello, Martin."

My former boss glanced toward the dining room. "I hope I'm not interrupting anything."

"Dinner. Care to join us? We made a roast."

"I'll pass, thank you. According to my wife, I'm a vegetarian this week. Anyway, this won't take long. The bureau wishes to extend its gratitude and requests your return to Hex Support in an official capacity."

I rolled my eyes. "Martin, I told you..."

He held up a hand. "I know, I know. I'm not asking for a full-time commitment, although we could use someone of your caliber. We'd be prepared to accept you on a consultancy basis. You choose the cases you'd be willing to accept."

The sound of my sisters' voices drifted from the dining room. Strong. Capable.

I focused on Martin. "This consultancy...What kind of qualifications would someone need to have?"

His brow creased. "What do you mean? You're a qualified agent."

"I know, but my sisters aren't."

He blinked rapidly. "You want Elizabeth and Grace to join Hex Support?"

Yes. Yes, I did.

"They're Fairfield witches. Their magic is unparalleled."

"I know, but you've always been so protective of them."

"They're smart, skilled, and powerful. They'd be an asset."

"No doubt," Martin murmured. "Let me speak to the higher-ups and I'll let you know."

I nodded. "Tell them my continued participation is contingent on it."

He tugged his ear. "I have to admit, I'm surprised that you of all people are asking to add family members to the roster. Are you certain?"

I didn't hesitate. "Yes. It's time." Dark Hollow was a sanctuary, not a prison.

His mouth pursed. "Well, I suppose things are about to get interesting."

I smiled back at him. "You have no idea."

———

Get to know Elizabeth in *Harvest Moon*, the next book in the series.

For more information on Annabel's books, check out her website at www.annabelchase.com.